Nothing Ever Happens in North Berwick

The Somali Pirate Adventure

Etherick Brown

To Ross + Aileen

Ethrick Broun
aka
Malky

ISBN-10:147756862X
ISBN-13:978-1477568620

DEDICATION

We remember Big Jack, Bruce, Jim Pearson and Gold Finger who are sadly no longer with us but are no doubt enjoying the hospitality of the big pub in the sky. Look out for Donny when your in there guys. Be his friend and buy him a drink.

A big Shout to Sir Frank Ogden presently not drinking due to ill health but still thought of fondly by his drinking buddies.

CONTENTS

ACKNOWLEDGMENTS

Thanks to Ian Steel, the older one age 80, who provided the illustrations for the cover. Proof that you're never too old to publish your first work.

Ian Steel, who now lives in Aberlady, is a self-taught artist experimenting with watercolours, oils, pencil, charcoal and pastels. He was born on the Mains Farm, North Berwick where his father worked with heavy horses as a ploughman. Art College was not a possibility and he spent his working life as a painter with W Seaton & Son. His leisure always included sketching subjects from Spanish bulls to ancient and historic buildings.

A big thanks Ian, Irene, the staff and the patrons of the County Hotel. Many of them appear in this book. They all helped to make a great backdrop for a good story.

Special thanks to Martin Gaughin, Jo Gibson and Ian Goodall for their assistance with proof reading. Between the three of them they identified more mistakes than I would care to admit. Any that appear will no doubt be down to my additions after they had strived hard to perfect it.

Thanks also to Trish for her help with the web stuff.

A couple of pints. That was the plan. On the face of it a simple objective but Scottish drinking plans are fluid and complex affairs. That aside, How far off course could the quest for a couple of beers in the quiet coastal town of North Berwick go? Two lagers, an assault on Somalia in search of pirates, the involvement of gangsters, terrorists, National Security Services and a packet of crisps please. That is surely stretching it a bit far. Forget the crisps then.

Please drink responsibly because even in a small town, like North Berwick, where nothing ever happens, an impulsive approach to alcohol can result in some seriously weird and unintended consequences.

A tale of drink, drunks and National Security.

1 - SUNDAY

Malky was forty nine years old. Well, at least he was for another six hours. Tomorrow was his birthday, the big five-zero, 50 years old. For fifty, physically he was in reasonable health. At 6'2" tall he was probably two stone over his recommended body weight. His 35" waist was too big for the 34" inch jeans he was squeezed into but too small for the 36" ones he had recently started buying. His height meant he could carry the extra weight without looking too fat as long as he didn't relax his stomach muscles too much. 36 years of binge drinking had however taken their toll. He was bald as a coot, the bags under his eyes were luggage class and he no longer had the 28" waist he possessed as a 21 year old. These things aside he considered himself lucky and tonight's luck included a free pass on the town courtesy of the fact his wife was staying in Hamilton.

Tonight's drinking partner was Watty. Malky had met Watty when they both bought second homes in the seaside town of North Berwick where they were partaking of a few beers that evening. The plan was a couple of drinks. It was a fluid plan in more ways than one. Fluid mainly because they knew it would not consist of just a couple of beers but probably gallons of fluid. The plan was also fluid because no night out really went to plan when drink was involved and tonight's plan had already been amended within two minutes of leaving the flats. Instead of turning left towards the County Hotel, their local haunt, they had turned right and swallowed a pint each in the bars at the Golfers, the Quarterdeck and the Blenheim. The plan to have a couple of drinks in the County had already gone awry in more ways than one. Not only had they exceeded the planned couple of pints but Malky was drinking lager. Normally a connoisseur of heavy beer he had decided on a whim to order a lager tops for his first pint. The warm September day, the humid evening, the sweat induced by the walk to the pub or John

Smiths being off in the Golfers may have influenced his decision but for whatever reason he was on the lager. He knew lager wasn't a good thing to drink. The makers claimed it was all hops and stuff but the reality was it was just a crazy chemical soup that knocked the shit out of your brain cells. That aside it was a refreshing drink and Malky was enjoying it. Watty was drinking lager too and he was a well educated chemist. If anyone should be aware of the chemical properties of lager he should, and he was, but like Malky he had started binge drinking in his early teens. He didn't quite have the 36 years experience Malky had but that was only because he was a couple of years younger. When he hit 50 he would possibly even be more experienced than Malky. Watty was well qualified to know the dangers of drinking lager but it didn't stop him drinking far too much of it.

The original plan had been aborted in favour of the hostelries in the west end of town but the rest of the drinking establishments in the west end of town had either a select membership, which excluded Malky and Watty, or were just too far away to walk. *"Let's go to the County for a couple of pints"* announced one of them. The other agreed. They had a plan.

        The County Hotel was bouncing. It was the holiday weekend and the hotel was fully booked due to a couple of golfing parties from Newcastle and a couple who were attending a wedding at the nearby MacDonald Marine Hotel. North Berwick had many attractions which made it popular and people with serious money owned some very large properties in the town. The Location by the sea on the Firth of Forth, the beaches, the scenery, the golf courses and the proximity to Edinburgh made it a very sought after place indeed. The couple attending the wedding were also from Newcastle but not from the same area as the Golfers. They had originally intended to stay at the MacDonald Marine Hotel but had delayed booking too long and finding it fully booked they had been left with the choice of booking a five star hotel in Edinburgh or staying at the nearby County Hotel in North Berwick. Logistics suggested The County Hotel was the more practical option. Reasoning that they would only be staying one evening they decided to try a night at the County.

The party of golfers had been there all week. North Berwick was at the centre of some of the greatest golf in Scotland. Its seaside location, top class condition and spectacular views provided a fantastic golf experience. The championship course at Muirfield was located in Gullane some 5 miles west of the town. This traditional links course was due to host the British Open Championship in 2013. The North Berwick Golf Club at the west end of the town was also a Club steeped in tradition. Dating from 1832 it was renowned for providing generous hospitality and a testing golf challenge. The course was also a traditional links, which started and finished at the clubhouse within the town. It wound its way along the Firth of Forth offering stunning views over white sandy beaches, islands and across to the hills of the East Neuk of Fife. The Glen Golf Club at the east end of town was another outstanding links course with arguably more spectacular views. The golfing parties were having a ball. The golf had been excellent and the hospitality of the golf clubs had been exceptional. The hotel owners had been looking after them extremely well too. In fact, County Hotel manager, Ian Steel had been looking after them too well. As hotel guests the licensing laws in Scotland allowed them to drink 24hrs a day. Taking a week out of their lives, away from their wives and families, for a golf holiday, dictated that they had to try and drink for as many of those 24 hours a day as they could. *'It was okay for them'* thought Ian, *'They only have to stay awake for a weeks holiday. Same as the last weeks holiday squad and the mob the week before that. To keep the residents happy I'm at it 365 days a year.'* Ian had had enough of binge drinking. He decided it was going to be his night off and he promptly hid from his residents leaving Nina his trusty barmaid to keep the customers happy whilst he got some well earned rest.

Nina had a good few years experience in the drinks trade both as an employee and a punter. It would probably be fair to say that she had even more experience of binge drinking than Malky or Watty. She was working her magic in the crowded bar pulling pints, dispensing shorts and pouring mixers. The tea time crowd were starting to leave. Hopefully soon it would just be the residents and the hardcore drinkers. Give it another hour and the younger ones would drift off to some of the other pubs as was the normal routine on a Sunday night. Another couple of hours and she could sit and enjoy a drink herself.

Brian Anderson had dropped in for a tea-time pint. It hadn't quite gone to plan. His evening meal time had come and gone hours ago. *"Just another for the road",* he announced. He was on halves now. Not English style half pint halves but Scottish halves as in spirits. The patter had been good tonight and anything he had planned was out of the window now. Home and sleep off the effects of alcohol he thought but not just yet. The new plan was maybe just another for the road and then home but his plan like all drinking plans was fluid.

Malky and Watty's new plan was going well. *"Two lagers"* announced Watty on arrival at the County Hotel. Malky was now in full lager mode having dropped the lemonade tops that had accompanied his earlier pints. A chemical induced hangover was now a certainty tomorrow but the morning was some hours away and with the morning came his birthday. So, he had a certain duty to see out the last few hours of his forties downing as many more lagers as he could before reaching his next major age milestone. He scanned the room. The bar was full of non-locals whom he deduced were residents and a splattering of regulars he recognised as fellow patrons of the establishment. He laughed to himself at the thought of being local. He had been born and bred in the West. He was what the locals referred to as a white settler. An incomer who had raised the house prices making it difficult for locals to purchase property in their own town. Malky had spoken to other so called white settlers who felt excluded by the indigenous population but he had always been made very welcome. The County Hotel had practically adopted him. He exchanged pleasantries with everyone. These locals were his friends. He reminded himself of a quote once made by an alcoholic workmate of his, Donny, who insisted *"it's not yir friend that buys you drink."* He had been awful pessimistic though and finally topped himself with an overdose of some medicinal pills. Malky took his pint from Watty, *"Cheers pal"* he shouted to make himself heard in the din. *'Quite ironic'*, he thought, *'that Donny's warning comes into my head when I'm taking a drink from a chemist who's a friend'*.

Watty and Malky squeezed in between Brian Anderson, who was sitting regaling a story about Russian holidays, and big Bradley Bone another white settler from Newcastle. White settler wasn't really an appropriate description of Bradley. He was more of a white squatter. He had initially arrived in North Berwick to conduct some sort of work at the nearby mushroom factory in Fenton Barnes and just never got round to going home. He had also been adopted by the County Hotel and was a permanent resident. Bradley was a bit of a mystery. He was a pipe lagger to trade and still did the odd lagging job but he seemed to just duck and dive picking up work here and there. Here being North Berwick and there being anywhere between North Berwick and Portsmouth. Bradley was a big boy At least six feet three with broad shoulders, dark hair and a small paunch possibly obtained through drinking too much beer and latterly Guinness. He was probably in his early thirties and his dark hair, strange accent and new boy in a small town status had allegedly meant a number of the young and not so young girls in North Berwick, who were that way inclined, had been introduced to Mr Bone. This had on occasions also cost him some heavy grief but whatever he did he also knew some serious people in the South Shields Area. Malky had previously joked that Bradley was either a major North East gangster doing dodgy jobs or he had fallen foul of a North East gangster and was hiding in North

Berwick. Bradley, who knew the truth wasn't quite as exciting and liked to keep a veil of mystery surrounding his past life, just smiled and revealed nothing. He liked being mysterious especially when the girls were intrigued by Mr Bone. Bradley, Malky and Watty were also members of the County Hotel darts team so they had more in common than just binge drinking. They indulged in the usual jibes, niceties and speculations about the nocturnal activities of Mr Bone. This was followed by darts team updates and rumours that Stevie Duncan was signing for the County. After agreeing this would be a coup Bradley, Malky and Watty became aware of Brian Anderson's conversation about Russian holidays.

"Yes it's the latest in action adventure holidays" continued Brian Anderson. The darts team trio weren't quite sure how they got drawn into this conversation but fairly soon they were engrossed. Whoever Brian had been talking to, they were gone but he had now pulled in a new audience which caused his drinking plan to become slightly more fluid and another half for the road was ordered to facilitate a further telling of his holiday discovery. This also meant the second of

Malky and Watty's couple of pints had to be ordered so they could listen to the tale. Their plan was still on course. Bradley Bone, whose only plan was to drink Guinness all night, duly ordered another whilst Nina ran around like a blue arsed fly pulling, pouring and dispensing. *"Somali pirates"* Brian Anderson continued. *"You get yourself into deepest darkest Russia and get in toe with the Russian mafia. They show you how to handle an AK47 and those big inboard machine guns that are fixed to boats. You get tons of target practice and trained in sea warfare. Once you're up to speed they sail you into Somali waters and when the pirates come to get you, you can blow them away."*

Malky was instantly enthralled by the idea. In two hours time he'd be fifty. He wasn't exactly past it but how much longer would he be able to claim that. Neither had his life been dull. He was a retired policeman, having left Strathclyde Police after serving 31 action packed years which had been challenging and exciting. At 18, naive and innocent of the ways of the world he had donned the uniform and was initially identified and earmarked for promotion. Prior to joining he was no stranger to alcohol but the drinking culture embedded in the police at the time and the pressure associated with his preferred line of work, criminal investigation, soon meant he had fallen foul of the drink and those involved in the promotion selection process. That was not necessarily bad news however. Freed from the politics of promotion he had dedicated his career to catching criminals. He was soon identified and groomed for a life in the various squads that do the business in this line of work. This meant working long hours and devising innovative strategies to ensure success. It included world travel and long periods away from home. It meant shit loads of overtime and large pay packets. It meant he never worked for less than a Chief Inspectors salary even though he only ever attained the rank of Detective Sergeant. It meant he continued to drink far too much and fitted in perfectly with the clientele of the County Hotel who had adopted him, just over a year ago, on his retirement from what he had considered the best job in the world. Shooting Somali pirates had a ring of justice about it. Administering the ultimate punishment to those parasites dealing, in kidnap, extortion, murder and rape fitted right in with his lawman ethos. This was a topic worthy of further conversation, *'we could have some fun with this'* thought Malky. *"Sounds fantastic, have your gangster mates got any contact with the Russian mafia, Bradley?*", he asked of Mr Bone. Brian Anderson smiled and promptly ordered another half. His drinking plan was now well and truly fucked. It wasn't the only one.

Bradley Bone and Watty were up for a laugh and they sensed Malky was too. Malky was famous for ripping the pish and starting ludicrous debates just to wind people up. Bradley and Watty decided to join in. Ideas and views on the pros and cons of what would be involved in a Somali pirate shooting holiday, run by the Russian mafia, began to bounce about the bar. Davy Kerr the darts team captain listened intently.

The big problem with the deal was the lack of guarantees. A mafia rip off was suspected. Give them a couple of hundred grand and they let you shoot a few bullets before taking you on an uneventful cruise where Somali pirates are as rare as last orders for residents in the County Hotel. It was decided that some guarantees would be required before any thought to signing up could be considered. A proper contract was probably needed but as the only contracts associated with the Russian mafia would probably mean a contract out on you, the whole Somali pirate shooting excursion was looking a dubious non starter. Then Davy Kerr had an idea. *"Look, fuck the Russian mafia. Cut out the middleman. Ian and I can train you"* announced Davy. North Berwick had several residents with military experience. Davy Kerr was one and Ian Steel was another. No one quite knew where Davy had served in the forces but Ian Steel took great delight in telling everyone that Davy had been in the catering corps. Davy wasn't too talkative about his military experience. Someone said he had been in the Gulf war but no one really knew. Army folk said the ones that talk about active service have never seen any whilst those who have, normally don't talk about it. Based on that premise Davy must have been Special Forces or something. He put Somali pirate shooting back on the starting blocks and the logistics of going freelance became the new topic of conversation.

It was decided Bradley and his shady contacts would sort out the guns and stuff. What quite stuff meant was never really disclosed but Bradley just nodded, winked and tapped his nose.

He had it sorted. No problem, the gear was got, *"Whay aye man, no worries!"*

Watty, with his chemistry set, was designated explosives officer with the task of making everything from fertilizer and other natural ingredients. *"Easy, it's a dawdle!"* announced Watty.

With the practicalities of the arsenal sorted, the matter of transport and logistics had to be solved. Benjy's fishing boat was suggested as the ideal craft to attract Somali pirates with possibly one of the North Berwick life boats as back up. Benjy Pearson was the local lobster fisherman and his boat puttered about between his pots on the Firth of Forth. No one knew what size it was but the general consensus was it would probably be able to get from North Berwick to Somalia via South Shields to pick up the arsenal nae bother.

"Ah don't think Benjy will give us it" someone voiced.

"Well we could borrow it" someone else suggested.

"But who would drive it" enquired another.

"Ah've got my Royal Yachting Association inland yachting certificate level two, a radio operator licence and an introduction to navigation course under my belt" boasted Malky who was now well aware the couple of pints plan was just about as far off course as he would be if he tried to pilot a boat to Somalia. He was getting light headed and there was still an hour to go until his birthday. *"Aye I'll have another"*, he beckoned to Watty who was racking up another round of drinks.

"Where the fucks Somalia?", voiced a voice.

"Eh! I think its in East Africa. Somewhere, near Madagascar" suggested Malky.

"Well, you need to know, I've just made you navigator" said Davy.

"Easy just head out there to the Atlantic", said Malky pointing in the direction of the North Sea."

"The Atlantics over there" stated Watty pointing to the toilets.

"OK, head through the channel and go round the pointy bit at the bottom of Africa and up the other side till we get there" declared Malky.

"That's the navigation sorted then and we can do all the weapons and tactical stuff on the open sea after we pick up the arsenal at South Shields" broadcast Davy

"What are we going to eat and who's buying the petrol" squeaked someone in the corner.

"It's a fishing boat and Ian's a cook" offered Davy.

"Ian doesnae like fish" said Nina

"Fuck him" grunted Davy *"He'll just have tae eat it and Malky you've a yachting badge, we'll rig up a sail on Benjy's boat and that'll save diesel."*

"What about the documentation to fool all the different Navy's and Coastguards we might run into along the way" asked Watty. *"Floating about in the South Atlantic or the Indian Ocean in a North Berwick Lobster boat, shooting fuck oot the place whilst stealing folks fishing quota's might draw us a bit of attention from the authorities."*

"Nina can shag them all", laughed Bradley. Mr Bone was rising to the challenge. *"If Nina gets on her back for a couple of coastguard cutters and the odd aircraft carrier they should turn a blind eye to our activities."*

"She might get sick of fish dinners too" giggled Watty.

"Nina we've a job for you" offered Malky and the boys took great delight in outlining Nina's roll in the operation.

"Maybe Durex will sponsor you" offered Mr Bone. Nina was not impressed but Bradley persisted. *"You only have to shag half the world's navies. You can practice on me."*

"That will be right" retorted Nina *"your not even fit to be called a wanker. Your hand even rejected you. Last time you tried, it fell asleep."*

"Aye you'd change your mind if I unleashed the trouser snake" boasted Bradley trying to regain the upper hand.

"Your two inch tadger and a cobra have certainly got one thing in common" suggested Nina. *"I wouldn't fuck with either of them."*

Watty nearly spilled his pint laughing at Bradley's expense.

Bradley disputed Nina's claim *"Two inches, it's more like twelve you should suck it and see."*

"Sod off I'd get foot in mouth then" replied Nina to

the amusement of Davy, Malky, Watty and Brian who were now engaged in raucous laughter. Bradley surrendered *"Fuck it's my round, you'll laugh on the other side of your face when the navy get you."* Like it or not Bradley had decided Nina was in. It was essential if the plan was to work. Nina racked up another round and two blondes sauntered into the bar.

Shemain and Theresa were good Irish girls. They were travelling through the area looking for opportunities. They were on route from the traveller site in West Boldon, Northumbria to the Carluke area of Lanark to visit relatives.

The two blondes were tidy. Watty was single, divorced and available. Mr Bone was there to back him up and Malky was there too. The conversation about guns, bombs, shooting folk and meeting with gangsters continued in the corner where Nina was still disgusted at the thought of servicing an entire aircraft carrier. In another half hour Malky would be fifty. He had read somewhere that sex seeking females did not look at men over 55. He still had five years and 30mins left before he was past it.

One of the blondes was looking distressed maybe he could help?

Theresa was 27 years old and aware of her looks. She looked around and saw a bar full of middle aged men. Plenty of opportunities here she thought looking at Shemain in that knowing way. Shemain nodded whilst also looking around. The tables occupied by the golfers were packed. Drink was abundant, cash was evident and the mood was merry. A group of guys were standing around the bar and they looked merry enough to be departed from their cash too. Shemain motioned to the bar and Theresa started crying.

Malky assessed the problem. The poor girls were stranded in North Berwick trying to get to Carluke to visit their sick mother who was ill in the Law Hospital. They were distraught and beside themselves with worry. They needed the train fare to Carluke and money for their hotel. Most of the hotels were full because of the holiday weekend and they had been forced to book into a hotel they couldn't afford. They had left a £50 deposit but faced another £100 bill in the morning. Malky smiled, hoping to appear sympathetic but really amused at the affront of these two rogues who had strong Irish accents and hadn't properly researched their scam. *"Poor Girls, what do you think Walter?"*

Walter thought one had a smashing pair of tits and the other had a cracking arse. He also recognised the accent and could smell something fishy. *"Law Hospital",* he murmured also realising the girls hadn't properly researched their scam. Malky noted Walter had cottoned on and thought it was time to move things to the next level. Law Hospital had been abandoned years ago. He had used its derelict buildings in various training exercises which allowed the police to practice techniques for rapid entry during drugs raids. The hospital was now a massive building site where new housing developments were springing up or would be if the economy could get back on track. Presently it was just a source of scrap metal thefts. One thing Malky did know about Irish travellers was that they are often involved in recycling scrap metals. Sixty percent of the raw material for Irish steel is sourced from scrap metal. Approximately fifty percent, roughly 75,000 metric tonnes, is collected and segregated by the travelling community at a value of over £1.5 million and percentages for more valuable non-ferrous metals were probably significantly greater. Malky and Watty offered to put the girls up for the night and drive them to Carluke in the morning. Watty even offered to run them there in his BMW convertible but no one offered the girls a drink. Within five minutes the girls had melted away into the company of the golfers. They weren't crying anymore and Watty and Malky were back planning an assault on Somalia.

Malky was suddenly grabbed by Nina who pulled him across the bar threw her arms around his neck and planted a big kiss on his lips. *"Fucks sake"* thought Malky *"She's taking the practice for aircraft carrier servicing quite seriously."* He considered doing tongues and having a quick grope but then he realised he was getting his birthday kiss. Before he knew it, he had a malt whisky in his hand. *"Congratulations"* voiced those in the know and *"Happy birthday old bastard"* reverberated around the room. He swallowed the whisky giving little thought to the state of his head in the morning, *"A couple of pints, that plan was well and truly fucked now."*

The attack came from behind. Watty probably started it, Bradley joined in and Davy reluctantly followed. Malky was seized by three assailants who weren't very well coordinated. Watty's plan had been to bring him down and hold him whilst they removed his trousers and underwear leaving Malky naked from the waist down in a crowded pub. As Malky tried to work out their plan he fended off his assailants to stay on his feet. He was happy to be a sport but until he fully understood their intentions that was a risky thing to do. Watty was now fumbling with Malky's trouser belt but was struggling to undo it. The others loosely held his arms. Bradley kicked at his leg as Davy pulled him and the four of them toppled to the floor. Malky decided to grab some insurance and grasped for Bradley's left testicle seizing a lump of flesh in his hand. Bradley winced as his inner thigh was squeezed and thought, *"Thank fuck he never got ma baws."* They were now grappling around on the floor. Who first saw and raised the swimming pool sized dog bowl was irrelevant. What was important was Malky was the one who dictated which way its contents spilled and that Watty and Bradley took the brunt of the soaking. Released from his captors Malky lifted himself from the floor and presented himself to Nina. *"They wanted my tackle out, why don't you do the honours"* he laughed raising his arms in the air to give her unfettered access to his manhood. Nina giggled and acted all coy but in ten seconds flat she had his trousers at his ankles and his meat and two veg on public display. Malky took the subsequent applause from the crowd, twirled to ensure they had got the most from the experience and bowed before returning his gear to the security of his trousers. Bradley and Watty tried without much success to wring out the dog bowl contents from their shirts and trousers. The conversation quickly returned to Nina and her reluctance to service an aircraft carrier despite the fact she had dis-robed Malky quickly enough. This factor was enough evidence for the boys to decide she was back on board. Nina just shrugged her shoulders. "*Men, if only vibrators could mow the lawn"* she thought.

The couple returned from their wedding at the Marine Hotel. It had been a good night. The wife had been enchanted by the whole affair. The lovely hotel with the turrets, the magnificent views, the happy couple, the romance, the atmosphere, the etiquette and the charming people had made her night. The noise from the bar attracted her attention, *"Come on dear we'll pop in for a night cap"* she suggested. Her husband was delighted at the prospect of another drink. The bar was crowded and there were no seats so the wife stood at the inner doorway leading from the bar to the stairs giving access to the rooms. She found herself standing behind Davy and big Bradley who had their backs to her.

"Right", Davy stated, looking at Bradley *"It's all sorted we get the guns from your underworld pals in Newcastle, We should get ammo there too."* He turned to Watty *"you can source the explosives."*

"Aye" beamed Watty *"I can get the stuff to make grenades, bombs, charges, everything to take out anything you want"*

Davy continued and looked at Nina *"You have all the equipment necessary to overcome any attention from the authorities and the transport is sorted."*

Nina gave Davy a disapproving look.

Bradley smiled and then butted in looking at Malky *"Aye and him being ex-Old Bill won't do any harm either. That should add to our credibility. Those* bastards *don't stand a chance we'll take out hundreds of them with all the guns and shit we're getting."*

They were all laughing now *"we can get moving next week then"* suggested someone.

The wedding wife was shocked. When husband came back from the bar he was promptly pushed upstairs to the room. The two gin and tonics he had purchased were swilling about in the glasses and he juggled to save the liquid nectar from spilling over the sides. He then decided a swig from each of them would help minimise spillage danger. He was ushered into his room and greeted with *"Terrorists, we're in the company of terrorists."*

'What on earths got into her now?' He mused. She had moaned about everything since she got here, in fact she had moaned about everything since he married her. He had been the product of a working/middle class family from South Shields but he had done well for himself in the dot.com boom and that had given him the money to move in the better circles but not the connections to open the doors to where the real power lay. That was where

his wife came in. She was part of the elite. Her family had contacts and friends in the government and they were connected to royalty. Her choice of husband had been frowned upon but he had finally been tolerated if not accepted by Daddy. His lower standing in the family had been reinforced by his disorganised approach to the wedding. His lack of foresight in not booking a room in the five star McDonald Marine Hotel had not been missed and his wife had moaned like the neurotic bitch she was. He quite liked this place but she found fault in everything. He didn't normally swear but he thought *'For fuck's sake woman, terrorists, are you out of your mind?'* Her attitude to this nice little hotel had been outrageous since he announced they were staying there. He had dismissed all her other frivolous complaints and now she had moved into fantasy complaints. Guys with guns and bombs were planning to kill hundreds of people and they were planning it in the bar. Complaining about the size of the shower or the spaces in the car park was one thing but claiming the world's leading international terrorists met in the bar for their conferences was outrageous, even by her standards. Like a good husband he agreed to investigate further. Get as much information as he could he was told, reconnoiter and survey. Get names, descriptions and listen to their plans. Uncle Rupert would need to know everything he could to thwart their operation. Uncle Rupert was something to do with the Civil Service and he was apparently well connected with the Foreign Office and MI6. Buy them drinks and loosen their tongues he was told. The first part was easy *'another G&T'*, he thought. It was always good to have a plan. He entered the bar which was now considerably quieter and emptier than before. The golfers were leaving and the crowd of guys who had been at the bar had left. Two blonde girls were eyeing him up and he thought they had obvious Irish accents. *"As good a place to look for terrorists as anywhere"* he thought *'and well the wife told me to buy them drinks'*. He turned to Nina. *"A large G&T please and whatever the young ladies are having."*

One look at the size of his wallet was enough to convince Shemain and Theresa to spirit the golfers off to bed and change targets. The golfers were convinced they had performed a good deed and the girls would he happy sleeping in their hotel in the knowledge that they could catch a train in the morning to visit their sick mother. The girls tried their magic on the man with the large G&T

and the even bigger wallet.

He wasn't getting anywhere. He had bought two rounds and all these two blonde Irish girls would talk about was their mum. Not a terrorist in sight, well apart from the two blondes trying to terrorise the cash from his wallet. He asked again about the guys at the bar. The blondes didn't know them but claimed they hadn't been enamoured by them. Old fuckers with disgusting habits they had been exposing themselves, rolling on the floor throwing water about and laughing all night.

"Terrorists, they were old farts and that was the limit to their explosive talents" snorted Shemain.

G&T man suspected their sick mum sob story might not be truthful and he considered that on any other night away he would probably have tried to exploit the situation, because they did look quite tidy, but not tonight as his wife was upstairs. He did not suspect for a minute that they were lying about the guys at the bar though.

Both girls had heard bits and pieces about guns and explosives but hadn't quite heard or understood what was being talked about. Theresa and Shemain knew better than to admit to knowing anything about anything especially when this cagey old prick was acting like a cop and asking about things people don't normally talk about. If he had only been trying to get into their knickers they could have went with that but the interest in guns and explosives had set off alarm bells. They could smell the authorities a mile off and this guy smelt bad. They played him along acting innocent and demure but signalled to each other it was time to go. Cousin Seamus would be sitting in his pick up on the outskirts of town waiting on tonight's pickings. Theresa flashed her cleavage again at G&T man whilst Shemain gathered their stuff together and they left. Theresa and Shemain were now convinced G&T man was Special Branch or some other kind of security scum. Their antics however had meant they had consumed free drink all night and obtained enough cash for two train fares they would never buy and the cost of a hotel room they would never book from twenty drunken Englishman. Oliver Cromwell would not have been proud of his countryman that night but then again hadn't Oliver Cromwell caused the problem in the first place?

The little stirring in his loins brought about by the Irish girls natural assets diminished at the thought of his neurotic, fat wife waiting upstairs for the results of his mission. He was convinced she was off her head. No one here knew anything about terrorists, he decided. He finished his G&T and headed upstairs thinking about Theresa's tits but he was quickly brought back into focus when reunited with his wife and he was berated for finding out nothing of importance. She told him she would phone Uncle Rupert and get him to sort it. Wishing he'd stayed for another G&T he persuaded her to sleep on it and contact Uncle Rupert in the morning. She made it abundantly clear sex was not on the menu and left him to wrestle with the images of the Irish girls. They would both have got it, it being a night of sordid sex. His mind drifted back to the wedding and he thought the bridesmaid would have got it too but then again so would the bride. That just wouldn't display etiquette though, would it? The idea of etiquette was quickly dismissed as he drifted off to sleep and experienced some strange erotic nightmare about Irish girls in wedding dresses trying to free his naked wife from the shower whilst she screamed for uncle Rupert to make the shower wide enough for her big fat ass.

Cousin Seamus soon met up with Shemain and Theresa. Like the perfect gentleman he was, he alighted from his vehicle and opened the passenger door for them. Shemain gave him a quick run down of the cash total for their nights work and alluded to secrets about weaponry and the Branch. He eagerly took his share of the nights haul and slapped the two girls firmly on the ass as they entered the pick up. *"Now what's all this talk about guns 'n' explosives and Special Branch?"* He asked.

2 - MONDAY

Uncle Rupert was up to his proverbial arse in alligators and they were snapping at his balls big style. The Monday morning Foreign Office meeting had covered a multitude of topics and most of the action points raised had landed on his desk. Libya, Syria and the Middle East were high on the agenda as usual. The euro crises continued and the Rugby World Cup with its resultant influx of Brits attending to spectate had raised a couple of logistical issues for the various British Embassies and Consulates in New Zealand. Several other security issues had been muted and discussed with the threat of terrorism always looming in the shadows. The various action points had to be offloaded and delegated to more junior staff but one issue had to be dealt with urgently and it wasn't one that had been raised at the meeting. His niece had been persistently calling since 9am that morning. His secretary had informed her he was busy but she was unrelenting. A matter of national security he had been told. He looked at the notes he had made during her phone call:

'Four or five guys and a woman had been drinking in a hotel in North Berwick, Scotland but he had no real descriptions of them or clues as to their identity other than one might be an ex-policeman and one had a Newcastle accent. They were accessing firearms and ammunition from underworld figures in the Newcastle area and one of them was an expert bomb maker. Whatever they had planned it involved killing hundreds of people and the transport to facilitate the operation was in place. It was due to happen next week and they had figured ways of negating or neutralising any intervention from the authorities.'

It was scary stuff, if it was true, but his niece was a little neurotic and prone to exaggeration. He couldn't however just ignore it. If he did and anything happened word would soon spread amongst 'the family' that she had told him and he would be criticised or even ostracised for doing nothing. That would not do his career any good at all. He made two phone calls. The first call was to the Security Services intelligence HQ at Thames House on Millbank in London. He spoke to another high ranking civil servant, outlined the nature of his intelligence, and authorised its entry into the intelligence system. The second call was to his opposite number in the Home Office. There was nothing international about this yet so it wasn't Foreign Office territory it would probably fall under the jurisdiction of SOCA, The Serious and Organised Crime Agency. He wanted a name to blame if this intelligence turned out to be true but was ignored until it was too late. He got his name and returned to the important stuff. *'What time was he lunching with his secretary?'*

His opposite number at the Home Office grunted. He now had the "no real provenance, low graded" bit of intelligence which carried with it high ranking interest. That was a bad combination. It was every intelligence operative's nightmare. He called a departmental head, briefed him and told him to check it out. The buck was passed again. He turned to his latest memo regarding scrap metal. A train operator wanted the law changed to tackle the rise in metal thefts. One copper cable theft from a railway line resulted in a total of 108 trains being delayed, 17 hours worth of hold-ups for thousands of passengers and damage estimated at over eighty thousand pounds. The value of the metal stolen probably netted the thieves fifty quid. Councils had reported streets being stripped of drain covers and supermarkets had lost hundreds of shopping trolleys in a matter of days. Letterboxes, charity clothing banks and door handles had also been taken. Scavenging for copper caused Napton in Warwickshire to lose telephone and internet services for nearly a week. Four metal goalposts were stolen in Horley, Surrey. Instruments worth £15,000 were taken from a town band in Pontarddulais in Wales. Shop letterboxes and door handles went missing in Durham and a children's slide was taken from a playground in Kent. Police had reports of wheelchair ramps being stolen and children's playgrounds being stripped. Blackpool's model village, a popular tourist attraction, had even been targeted. Scrap metal theft was becoming Britain's most annoying crime. Terrorists would have to wait, this was the priority.

Cousin Seamus had also been interested in spreading the word about the men in North Berwick who had guns and bombs readily available in Newcastle. He phoned his uncle Dermott who was in his caravan at the West Bolton travellers site. Uncle Dermott promised Seamus a few quid if the information proved useful. He knew just the man to turn this sort of info, scant as it may be, into cash. He had just finished his call to cousin Kieran in the South of Ireland and had been assured that if anything came of it he would be rewarded when word reached him that some bastard had stolen the wrought iron gates from the front of the traveller's site. *"Fir fucks sake is nothing sacred?"* He screamed.

By midday word of guns, bombs and North Berwick had reached the higher echelons of the former IRA Southern Command and was passed on to former members of the Dublin Brigade for the attention of the former IRA Quartermaster General. The intelligence system within the criminal underworld was proving to be more effective than those in the security services.

Somewhere around midday Malky stirred. His head was bouncing and he immediately regretted the lager frenzy that had caused it. He felt the pain emanating from the base of his skull and was reminded it wasn't just a lager frenzy that caused the pounding. There were several malt whisky's banging away in there too. His guts however felt fine. Upset stomachs were worse than headaches. He was a staunch believer in natural remedies and never touched any kind of headache tablets. Work off the headache he thought. *'Naw fuck it another half hour'* and he rolled over with the intention of another snooze. The familiar ring tone of a message arriving on his mobile brought him back to full consciousness. He grasped for the phone and brought his eyes into focus on the screen. 'Message from Marion' it displayed. "What ye doin" the message asked. He remembered, not that he had ever forgotten but he had been denying the fact that the real reason for his unsupervised presence at the flat was, he was meant to be working on restoring and redecorating it. Item one on the list was the thirty odd foot high wall that bordered the buildings at the rear. Along with Watty he had reclaimed the brick strewn, tree growing, derelict outhouse area located at the rear of the terrace and turned it into the Admiral Bar.

The area had been cleared and the bricks from the derelict outhouse had been used to mono block the ground. Two sheds had been erected giving much needed storage space and the area was now a nice little suntrap bordered by four high walls, the highest of which looked a bit dodgy. A window ledge was built into one of the walls which had been referred to as the bar because the cans and bottles from the numerous beers, consumed during the building process, had always rested there. The wood surrounding on the bar was painted admiral blue and the window ledge became known as The Admiral Bar after the colour of the Weathershield paint which had been discounted to four pounds ninety nine in the nearby Turnbulls hardware shop. All the walls needed pointing. About 6 bags of cement and 12 bags of sand had already been shoved into the walls but a lot more was needed. The top of the highest wall needed attention desperately and a storm was coming. Some big hurricane had devastated America and the winds were heading for Scotland. If the wall wasn't fixed it could blow over onto the nice new sheds. Malky texted Watty, they had better make a start or Marion would kill him. He checked his watch it was 1pm.

Giles Wainwright stared at the report on his desk. Educated at Trinity College in Cambridge he fulfilled all the criteria for a job in the security services. His analytical skills were second to none and he looked for clues in the report. It originated from the Foreign Office which was worrying. No security service gave away good intelligence if they could act on it. Information was power. This was probably poor intelligence but someone high up the tree wanted it followed up so it was a puzzle. He scanned the report. 'Four or five guys and a woman had been drinking in a hotel in North Berwick, Scotland but he had no real descriptions of them or clues as to their identity other than one might be an ex-policeman and one had a Newcastle accent. They were accessing firearms and ammunition from underworld figures in the Newcastle area and one of them was an expert bomb maker. What ever they had planned it involved killing hundreds of people and the transport to facilitate the operation was in place. It was due to happen next week and they had figured ways of negating or neutralising any intervention from the authorities. Giles came to a decision. The two obvious starting places were Newcastle and North Berwick but the last sentence worried him. If the authorities had been compromised the enquiries would have to be conducted discreetly. He couldn't go via normal channels with this. It would have to be kept in house. It would be restricted to the Special Branch or the Counter Terrorist Intelligence Section as it was now more commonly known. He looked up the numbers for his relevant contacts in the Northumbria and Lothian and Borders Areas.

Malky had raised Walter by now and both of them were precariously balanced on a ladder and a hastily rigged home made scaffold at the top of a thirty foot wall plastering cement into the spaces between the bricks. The wind was rising and howling through the trees. They concluded it wasn't the safest place to be, especially hung over and feeling like shite. Neither would admit to the other that they were scared or not up for the job so they soldiered on until the pointing was finished. The wind was blowing hard but the biggest danger to their balance was the giggling and laughing caused by the recollection of the previous night and all the nonsense they had talked about hunting Somali pirates. "*I wonder how big Benjy's boat is?*" They mused. When the job was done, it was nearly 5pm and tonight was darts night. The latest rumour was Ian Steel was tapping Stevie Duncan from "the Dally" or Dalrymple Inn to organise a transfer to the County Darts Team. "*C'moan lets get changed and go for a pint*" suggested Watty. "*Good idea*" replied Malky, happy now he had something positive to report to Marion. The wall was now hurricane proof and they had a plan. They might even have a new star in the darts team.

Giles Wainwright had not expected any great results from his initial enquiries and he wasn't disappointed. Newcastle had criminals and it had various criminal factions but the only real English based gangs were motivated by football. The Newcastle Gremlins and the Sunderland's Seaburn casuals were really the only English gangs in the Newcastle area. The old fashioned gangsters feared and reviled by everyone they met and living up to their reputations as dangerous criminals were a thing of the past along with their empires which had been built up from protection rackets, armed robberies and extortion. Crime (UK) Ltd was under new management. It was now largely foreign owned. Police across Britain were grappling with a new generation of criminal 'kingpins', whose empires spanned the globe and who modelled their operations on legitimate multinational companies. While the "dons" of the past revelled in their notoriety, displaying their ill-gotten gains through sharp suits and flash cars, today's gang leaders aimed to be faceless "executives" as familiar with spreadsheets as their predecessors were with knuckle-dusters. Foreign nationals, including Russian, Albanian and Turkish gangs, now had a stranglehold on organised crime in the UK. The information in the report could easily relate to a foreign mob which made the fact the Foreign Office had passed it on more disturbing. *'When was the next Newcastle v Sunderland match?'* He wondered. *'Were the Gremlins and the Seaburn casuals aiming to take football violence to a new level? That would keep it within Home Office jurisdiction'.* He checked his computer just in case. The first game had already been played and the 3rd March was the next local derby. That wasn't next week. He could discount that. Hopefully he'd hear something positive from his Scottish enquiries.

Watty and Malky were back in the County Hotel for the serious business of Monday night darts. The North Berwick and District Coastal League was a highly competitive league and the

County Hotel team took their darts seriously. So did tonight's opposition, the Auld Hoose, who were last season's champions. This was the second pre season friendly between the teams. The County had trounced them last week in the Auld Hoose and tonight the Auld Hoose wanted revenge. Ian Steel's attempts to tap Stevie Duncan hadn't yet been successful but Sheepy, the Auld House captain, had been working hard behind the scenes to ensure his team had an advantage. Bolstered by several ringers from West Barnes, the winners of the summer league, Sheepy and big Craig, a 'Mak'em', who originated from Sunderland and ran the Auld Hoose pub, led the Auld Hoose to victory. During the Match Watty hit a 180 and Malky notched up a 140 but they both got beat. Interspersed amongst the County's darts banter were recollections of the previous night and more nonsense about Somali pirates. People were frequently sent to the bar to get some good service from Nina 'the harlot of the seas' who was fed up receiving text messages to that effect.

Game over it was back to the bar and another round of drinks was ordered. The round system which was often blamed for Scotland's drink problems came into play and ensured no one was going home soon. Three Guinness and three lagers were promptly ordered as Malky, Watty, Davy and Bradley Bone were joined by Ian Steel and Pablo. Ian Steel was quizzed about the Stevie Duncan rumours but Somali pirates took centre stage again. Both Ian and Pablo had heard some of the ramblings about the Somali pirate story. Pablo was up for a laugh and decided to join in whilst Ian was more interested in keeping the congenial atmosphere in the bar. Once again the patter started, only this time they talked as if the trip was planned and not just a fantasy holiday. Davy outlined the training programme whilst highlighting Bradley's role in supplying the weapons and ammunition. Watty described the various explosives he could manufacture and deploy whilst Malky declared the cause was just and a worthwhile venture to undertake. *"We'll show these Somali bastarding pirates what justice is all about when we pop them"* he declared.

Andy couldn't believe his ears. Andy had been one of the golfers who had been in the bar the night before. He had thought these were all decent lads who liked a laugh. He had witnessed the hijinks of the previous evening when the dog bowl was toppled and one of them had their trousers removed. The din in the bar had drowned out their conversations though and he had been blissfully unaware of the Somali pirate banter. Now all he heard was talk of murder and he couldn't believe his ears. This was the final night of Andy's stay at the County. It had been a great few days and a real tonic for him. Andy worried about the world and in particular he worried about the future prospects for his grandson. Life in some parts of Tyneside was now all about gangs, violence and drugs. He always tried to guide his grandson properly keeping him away from violence, drugs and the wrong company. These guys at the bar all seemed to be decent people. He couldn't sit and listen to this talk of murder without trying to explain what a silly idea it was and how it could affect their families. Live and let live was his philosophy. These idiots at the bar didn't know what they would be letting themselves in for. He would have to reason with them. Andy thereafter became part of the Somali pirate discussion.

Malky, Bradley and Watty were giggling like schoolboys. They couldn't believe the nice old man was taking them seriously. He actually thought they were planning an attack on Somali pirates. The right and proper thing to do would have been to put the old boy out of his misery and put his mind at rest but after a few beers Malky, Bradley and Watty were far from sensible. They couldn't resist ripping the pish out of the old boy and the fantasy story was embellished and distorted out of all proportions.

Davy and Pablo who had never been known to miss out on a good wind up joined in with great gusto. The only one in the party who acted with any decorum was Ian Steel mainly because he had not been party to the original discussion on Somalia but more likely because he did not like the locals taking advantage of the residents. Even so, he became embroiled in the debate and took Andy's side in the argument. Andy insisted they were far too old and inexperienced to take on such a task. Davy disagreed highlighting Ian's and his own military background. He alluded to Malky's experience in dealing with organised gangs, Bradley's involvement and contacts in the underworld and Watty's expert knowledge of explosives. He gave the impression this was just another venture like many others they had carried out in the past. Malky tried to give Pablo some credibility. *"Pablo is a professional driver"* he announced referring to his previous employment as a taxi driver.

"That'll be fuckin useful" snorted Watty *"A wheelman in the middle of the Indian Ocean."* They all giggled like schoolboys again.

Andy was about to interrupt but Malky got there first. He objected to Ian taking part because he had sniper skills which would ruin the holiday for the rest of them. *"If that bastard pops them all from 1000yds before we get a chance on the AK47's it won't be much fun for the rest of us"* he muted.

Andy was now beside himself *"That's murder you're taking about. Those Somali are poor people with no other means of earning a living"* he scowled.

Malky sensed a liberal, left wing argument being voiced and adopted a staunch right wing view. *"They're scum causing misery and suffering and we're not allowed to shoot our own scum. The law won't let us, so we're off to Somalia to do our bit for crime and justice."* He offered.

Andy had had enough and he stormed off to bed. Ian was upset because he reckoned he could hit his target, with a sniper rifle, from at least 2000yds and the argument continued until all the drinks in the Scottish round system had been purchased and consumed or possibly longer. The plan was fluid after all.

3 - TUESDAY

The former IRA Quartermaster General had several things to think about. Business was brisk. The demise of the British in Northern Ireland was always at the forefront of his mind but activities like racketeering, bank robbery, drugs, and kidnapping concerned him too. A shortage of firearms, explosives and ammunition was affecting his operations as Turks, Kurds, Russians and Chinese invaded Dublin for a slice of its drugs trade. The Chinese in particular were causing problems to his organisation because of a misunderstanding. Whilst he had once ruled supreme he was now just another player in the global crime market. Another war was needed to unite the Irish but the enemy was now so globalised that focusing on the British would be stupid when all these other nationalities were doing far more damage to his country. He remembered fondly the good old days prior to the Good Friday agreement when he had an arsenal of weapons at his disposal. These included; 1,000 rifles, 3 tonnes of Semtex, 20-30 heavy machine guns, 7 surface to air missiles, 7 flamethrowers, 1200 detonators, rocket propelled grenade launchers, 100 handguns and 100 plus hand grenades. Now he was struggling to get his hands on a pea-shooter. He knew that not all of the IRA weaponry had been destroyed in the peace process and that he himself had been responsible for the removal of a very large cache of weapons from the negotiated deal. This weaponry could have equipped a small army and amongst tight security he had arranged for these weapons to be secreted in the vicinity of a secluded lake. The security had been so tight that only 4 men had been trusted with the location of the cache which, with a little expert outside help, had been hidden in a way that dogs, x-rays, aircraft and satellites could never find. Unfortunately they were all allegedly killed in a serious road accident before they could divulge the location to him. He suspected the British Special

Forces had been involved in the elimination of his men but this had never been proved. Other factions could also have been responsible but he believed the cache remained undiscovered even although his attempts to find it had been unsuccessful. The people who had helped him hide it were very upset that the cache could not be located. He thought it ironic that the people hired to ensure something could not be found were upset that it was now lost but he knew the reasons why they were upset and he also knew he would pay a high price if the cache was found by anyone other than his team or the hired help. Various people including the British Special Forces and a number of foreign firms, including the Chinese, were still prevalent in the area which was a sure sign no one had found the cache, although everyone denied looking for it. The area was secluded but numerous properties adorned the lake shores and he knew the team responsible for hiding the cache had been operating from a particular lakeside retreat. The property had been unoccupied at the time and borrowed by the IRA without the knowledge of its owner. He noted this property was coming up for auction and his contacts had made him aware of all the prospective buyers. His old IRA intelligence networks were still in place and a strange coincidence was evident. Up until now he had never heard of North Berwick in East Lothian, Scotland but in the space of hours, two different reports concerning the small seaside town had come to his attention. The first from the background checks on one of the buyers of the lakeside retreat highlighted he was in the habit of purchasing euro from the post office in North Berwick and the second was from contacts in the travelling community who believed some mob there had acquired a large amount of ammunition, explosives and firearms. This was too much of a coincidence to overlook. This particular house was attracting a few buyers from various locations but suddenly the North Berwick angle merited further investigations. He made the necessary arrangements and selected two operatives for the task.

Rab purchased four thousand pounds worth of euro from the post office and then decided it was time for a drink. A dark rum and Coke at his old army pal's hotel would suit him nicely. He checked his watch. It was eleven o'clock on the button. The pub would be open. He was off to Ireland tomorrow to try and buy a house but he had no more business today other than to get himself a room and a couple of dark rums. Armed with a plan he headed for the County Hotel.

Andy, the golfer, had left North Berwick at 9am that morning. He was still deeply concerned about the intentions of the mercenaries, as he now perceived them to be, who were intent on heading to Somalia for what they considered a bit of sport. The idea that they may even be sourcing their weapons from Tyneside caused him even more heartache. On his return home the first person he wanted to see was his grandson. His grandson was working but he met him in a South Shields coffee shop where they took a seat in an alcove. This coffee shop was owned by a Romanian and part of the attraction was the high partitions between the alcoves which gave each table and its patrons the illusion of privacy. It was very popular with dating couples, businessmen and anyone who didn't like looking at their fellow diners. Andy began to relay the story about the mercenaries he encountered in North Berwick and their ludicrous idea of fun. Andy being just a little deaf found it difficult to keep his voice down although he tried.

Joey Carr would probably be best described as a weasel, like those portrayed in 'the wind and the willows'. He was evil, greedy and an enemy of Toad Hall, If Toad Hall were the general public. He was a predator and displayed just enough cleverness and guile to endure his meagre existence in the only world he knew, the world of the underclass. Joey's drug dealer had just left. They had met in this particular coffee shop with its alcoves because they gave a degree of privacy where they could do a bit of business out with the prying eyes of the public and the police. There were no security cameras inside and the owner, while not openly encouraging any illegal actions, did his best to create an environment where discreet deals could take place. Joey would give his dealer five minutes to clear the area then he would leave. He lifted his cup to swallow the last of his coffee when he became aware of the conversation in the next cubicle. His attention was honed when he heard *"AK47"* he listened to try and catch the rest of the conversation but the music in the café was loud and he struggled. He stuck his ear to the partition and listened as attentively as he could;

"They are from North Berwick" …. *"They are after Somali"* … *"going by boat"*… *"They're getting guns and explosives"* ….. *"Bomb maker"* ……

"Coming to Tyneside"……. "Somali" …… "Killing hundreds   of people"….."Snipers"…….."AK47"….."Benjy's boat"…. "It's happening next week"

He would have tried to hear more but the waitress arrived at the table. Paranoia gripped him and he decided it was time to go. He had an appointment with a drug high just as soon as he got out of here. He would have to be careful. He was no stranger to the law and he had been jailed two weeks ago for possessing cocaine. The Old Bill had threatened to lock him up forever if he didn't grass up some of his mates and he had spilled the beans about a few things. They had also offered him some cash for more information then followed that up with a few threats on what would happen to him if he didn't keep in touch. Joey would keep this one up his sleeve in case the Old Bill got back on his case. He peered out the door and headed into the street.

When Andy unburdened his soul, his grandson laughed. As Andy had relayed the story it just sounded so stupid and it didn't actually seem a reality now. On reflection he now suspected that the idiots from the County Hotel might actually have been taking a rise out of him. The more he related the story the sillier it seemed. He sniggered to himself as the realisation hit him. What they were talking about was ludicrous and he had been lured into their joke. He had fallen for it hook, line and sinker. He decided he would book in to the hotel again next year and extract his revenge. The whole North Berwick scene was just too good to miss out on and the jokers in the County Hotel were certainly characters. Next year he would show them. He asked his grandson to help him write a positive review of the hotel and his experience on trip advisor the internet hotel review website. It had been a tremendous week and North Berwick plus the County Hotel had been an outstanding combination for a golf holiday. He thought about how he had been taken in by the wind up merchants in the pub. What a twit he was!

Jamie Douglas and Bill Elliott were two Northumbria Police neighbourhood beat managers. That was the latest name given to police constables involved in community policing initiatives in the war against crime. Today they were operating in plain clothes harassing the local junkies who were causing some bother in the Shields. One of them spotted Joey Carr. *"Let's have him"* suggested the other and poor Joey subsequently found himself in an interview room within Millbank Police Station. Jamie Douglas and Bill Elliott couldn't believe their ears. Their initial search had recovered a deal of cocaine, a slither of cannabis and two blues commonly known as valium or diazepam tablets. It wasn't the haul of the century but for these two young officers, it was a result. This was the second time in three weeks they had caught Carr and they listened intently as Joey tried to barter his way out of prison with tales of guns, explosives and bullets which were headed from South Shields to North Berwick for some hit on a Somali mob who were trying to establish themselves there. He embellished the story to make it more interesting. PC Jamie Douglas was not convinced but he was aware of an ongoing feud between the notorious Conroy and O'Malley crime families in Tyneside and sort of misinterpreted the implications of the information. Did you say Somali or O'Malley he asked? Joey panicked, he needed to get out. He couldn't stand a night of cold turkey suffering withdrawal symptoms in a police cell with nothing more than a couple of Librium obtained from the police doctor to control his anxiety. He told the inexperienced police officer what he wanted to hear and a very informative report found its way into the intelligence office at Northumbria Police Headquarters.

Giles Wainwright checked out the report which had landed on his desk at the Security Services intelligence office. Numerous frauds were perpetrated every day in the UK costing millions of pounds which often financed terrorism and organised crime. Banks were often the victims and this report related to the Post Office, one of the major UK banks and activities at a Preston call centre. It came to his attention mainly as a result of him flagging any intelligence relative to the small town of North Berwick in East Lothian, Scotland. An Asian call centre worker had been caught selling details of customers transactions, including one particular customer who had purchased euro at the North Berwick Post Office. The recipients of the information were believed to be linked to the IRA namely former members, if there was such a thing, of the Dublin Brigade. Giles scratched his head. Bombs and bullets in North Berwick with IRA interest, maybe there was something in this intelligence. Did this make it Security Service's (MI5) or Secret Intelligence Service's (MI6) jurisdiction? Dublin was foreign soil. If he could prove it was an IRA plot it was out of the security services jurisdiction unless the target of the attack was mainland Britain. He had no real evidence of either so he decided to continue his own enquiries keeping it very much in the domain of the security services. He picked up the phone.

Rupert Basingstoke had enjoyed a very pleasant lunch at his club. The cigars were excellent and the brandy was divine. He was discussing the progress of an ongoing intelligence operation involving some of the many MI6 personnel that were deployed around the world. Operation Chameleon had been running for over 6 years now and was starting to produce results. Rupert liked to rely on good old fashioned proper intelligence gathering methods. Agents on the ground provided good intelligence. The modern methods of technical surveillance, be it via phone tapping, CCTV, tracking, e-mail interception or satellite surveillance were useful but they were no substitute for proper agents in the right places. His company Blackberry vibrated in his pocket. Open use of mobile phones was frowned upon in the club. The use of any unencrypted communication devices was frowned upon by the Secret Service.

The Chinese, the Russians, the Americans, the Israelis and even the god dammed French could find his exact whereabouts by tracking an unencrypted phone. His phone was untraceable and so should he be but his infernal portly niece was still persuading his secretary to forward enquiries about his progress in thwarting the terrible intentions of her North Berwick terrorist cell. He really should reprimand his personal secretary but she really did enjoy the personal aspect of her occupation. Her reprimands could be interesting too. *'Spanking'* he thought before returning to the issue of Operation Chameleon.

Rab was enjoying his eighth dark rum and Coke or maybe it was his ninth. He checked his watch it was 4.30pm. The after work regulars were beginning to fill the bar of the County Hotel. Spocky, the mechanic, and Bruce, the deliveryman, were in their usual seats beside James the joiner, ex-navy Glen and Mick the retired engineer. Benjy, the fisherman, was sitting in his seat by the window talking to Wullie the local plumber. Scot the roofer was sitting on a stool by the bar conversing with Dougie, the taxi driver. Stevie Duncan, the oil worker, was also in the bar which fuelled the rumours Ian Steel was trying to tap him for the darts team. Craig was working hard behind the bar ensuring everyone had a full glass. Tomorrow Rab would be heading for Dublin to hopefully purchase a secluded lakeside retreat with 15 acres of land. It needed a bit of work and was extremely isolated but with a little love and attention it could be his paradise. The housing market across the whole of Europe was in decline due to the flailing economy and the euro crisis meaning the careful speculator could pick up a real bargain. Rab hoped to pick this place up for around sixty thousand euro but he would go to eighty thousand if necessary. He had already been outbid at two previous auctions in Poland and Lithuania so this time he might have to be a bit more realistic with his bidding. Tomorrow he would be in Dublin for Friday's auction and by Monday he hoped to be the laird of some isolated Irish estate.

Rab wasn't the only one heading for Dublin. In Kurdistan instructions were issued and three extremely dangerous and professional looking gentlemen, accompanied by a rather small unobtrusive man, left to head for Arbil International Airport.

Charlie Brandon worked in a Divisional Intelligence Office servicing Northumbria Police. He looked at the latest intelligence report concerning the feud between the notorious crime families headed by John Harry O'Malley and Patrick Conway. The O'Malleys were sourcing guns, ammunition and explosives from a mob in North Berwick, Scotland to use in a mass killing spree in Tyneside. He googled North Berwick. It was all adverts for golf, hotels and visitor attractions. He checked Wikipedia. *"The Royal Burgh of North Berwick is a seaside town in East Lothian, Scotland. It is situated on the south shore of the Firth of Forth, approximately 25 miles east of Edinburgh. North Berwick became a fashionable holiday resort in the 19th century because of its two sandy bays, the East (or Milsey) Bay and the West Bay, and continues to attract holiday makers to this day. Golf courses at the ends of each bay are open to visitors."* It certainly didn't look like the arms trafficking centre of the universe but further reading revealed that possibly only arms dealers could afford to stay there *"North Berwick consistently appears at the top of national house price surveys, and like for like prices are comparable to Edinburgh. North Berwick was listed as the most expensive seaside town in Scotland in*

2006, and was second to St. Andrews in 2009." He checked the grading of the intelligence it was graded B3 which meant it was from a source that had in the past proved to be accurate but the information was not known to have originated from the source. The source had acquired the information from a third party but it was believed to be true. Charlie Brandon had level seven security clearances which meant he could check the provenance of the source and the identity of the submitting officer. Jamie Douglas was the copper who had submitted it. He was an arrogant little shite in the neighbourhood team. He wasn't the brightest and his information had never really provided any results. He checked the source and found it was Joey Carr. That little weasel like, crack head Joey would sell his granny for drugs. There was no way he could be privy to any useful information regarding O'Malleys sourcing weaponry. Joey had overheard the conversation in a Romanian owned coffee shop. He couldn't identify the source. Charlie Brandon's professional opinion was that this was not intelligence but unverifiable nonsense. Procedures dictated however that he had to record it. He downgraded the intelligence rating to C4 which equated to an unreliable source where the reliability of the information cannot be judged. No other action was to be taken other than marking it for the information of The Lothian and Borders Police Service who covered the picturesque seaside town of North Berwick. To fit in with force protocols the message was sent to the security services who would access his recommendation and decide if it was cleared for onward transmission. The report was then filed in the Force Intelligence database.

Malky was on dog walking duty. North Berwick was a stunning place to walk. The views across the Forth were outstanding and he could see several of its islands which were clearly visible from the town. He checked out Fidra, The Lamb, Craigleith, and Bass Rock. He headed along the West Beach towards the harbour. A number of yachts were moored in the bay. The harbour was full of boats and numerous people were having meals or coffees at the Lobster Shack outdoor café. The recently developed Scottish Seabird Centre near the harbour was also busy with visitors all eager to observe the thriving colony of birds, including puffins, gannets, and other seabirds which occupy the very white looking Bass Rock. This was due largely to the gannets and their guano that covers much of its surface. The rock wasn't really white it was covered in bird shit.

He walked past the two resident ice cream vans which were a permanent fixture during the high season. Mr Whippy and the S Luca vans had caused many a debate amongst their patrons over who sold the best ice cream. Then it was onto the golden sands of the East Bay and past the outdoor swimming pool where Max his faithful West Highland Terrier bounced into the sea. On his exit a violent shake of his coat sprayed seawater all over the place as they dawdled along the golden expanse of sand and headed for the Glen. The waves which often enabled some decent surfing were rolling in towards the beach. The Glen golf course looked magnificent. Its club house overlooking the sea provided awesome scenery for its diners. They headed up the Glen walkway along the banks of the small stream that flows through there. This walk had been described by Robert Louis Stevenson as "the ladies walk" in an essay titled "the Lantern Bearers" which had been written in 1888 about a certain easterly fisher-village which was created seemingly on purpose for the diversion of young gentlemen. The Glen had once been the location of the Mills of Kintreath which had been built there in 1434 and latterly the Waulk Mill which had been built in 1738. The mills hadn't been used since the 1840's but ruins were still visible in the Glen. Walking out of the Glen, they entered the playing fields which were also home to the North Berwick Rugby Club. They crossed the playing fields heading past the tennis courts, putting green and Strings Café before entering the North Berwick Lodge grounds. The Lodge had recently won a Green Flag award. They recognise and reward the best parks in the country and the lodge grounds stood out after impressing the judges with its excellent use of green space, well-maintained facilities and high standard of safety and security. They walked past the swing park, café and aviary before stopping at the back door of the County Hotel. *"Dog'll be thirsty thought Malky"* and they popped in for a quick drink.

Benjy, the fisherman, was enjoying a Guinness with Wullie, the plumber who was enjoying a lager. Malky had a joke with them about the Somali pirates story and questioned if Benjy's boat was up for the job. *"Aye we could make it if we headed for France and went through the canal systems into the Mediterranean. Then if we went down through the Suez Canal into the Indian Ocean"* offered Benjy. Malky ascertained the name of Benjy's Boat but very quickly forgot it as he was cornered by Rab who was now on his tenth or was it his eleventh or maybe it was his fifteenth dark rum and Coke. Rab gave him a quick rundown on his Dublin trip and Rab interrupted. Dublin Rab was instantly dubbed Rab two by rocker Rab who claimed the rights to Rab one or real Rab. Rab two was too drunk to care and headed for bed. Rab one started on the high fives and reverse handshakes before announcing he was having a 55th birthday celebration on Saturday in the County where all were welcome. Malky finished his Guinness and left. He tried to remember the name of Benjy's boat. Was it Delta Queen or Delta Girl? It was definitely Delta something!

Tuesday was drawing to a close but PC Jamie Douglas was still on the case. He was now off duty and drunk in Roxanne's night club. He was trying to impress a rather tasty blonde beauty with the most amazing tits he'd seen since the last time he'd donned the beer goggles. Sally was more portly than shapely but she was attractive in as much as she looked available. Jamie reckoned he'd impressed her. The lass's liked the 'bizzies' and he was a top copper. He was well 'mullered' as they say in Newcastle and the effects of being drunk were causing him to break the Official Secrets Act in the active pursuit of this young girl's virtue. Sally listened intently as he told her about his role in bringing down the two most notorious crime families in Tyneside. Her interest in O'Malley and Conway spurred him on and the story got enhanced in proportion to her tits which were growing exponentially with every drink he consumed. Oh he wanted to pump this lass so hard. Unfortunately for Jamie the only pumping he got was Sally pumping him for information, which he readily exposed. He was so drunk and disorientated he even gave away the name of his informant because he thought it made him look impressive and important. At the end of the evening he was penniless, mortal drunk and alone. Sally had however uncovered a few things, including information about drugs and explosives heading for Tyneside, which would be very useful to her uncle who would be very interested in the activities of Messer O'Malley and Conway. She also had young Jamie Douglas's mobile phone number.

.

4 - WEDNESDAY

Giles Wainwright was in the Home Office Security Services intelligence room at 7am sharp. Commuting was a nightmare and to beat the traffic an insanely early start was required. He logged onto his computer and began sipping his first coffee of the day. This would be the first of many to be drunk that day. Coffee was his only vice and he loved it. 12 cups a day was normal. On a bad day he could swallow as many as 18 cups, it all depended on the workload and the stress. Scanning his e-mail inbox, one message immediately jumped out. It was headed 'Intel report 13092011s56783 from Northumbria to GHQ for consideration of Lothian and Borders Police

North Berwick.' The Security Services had unrestricted access to most intelligence databases and the police were fairly low on the national security pecking order. By flagging his interest of matters relating to North Berwick he was receiving numerous reports of traffic offences that had been committed or reports on domestic violence between estranged couples in the area but this was a direct link between Tyneside and North Berwick. He opened the email and read through its content.

"There is currently an ongoing feud between two families in the Northumbria Police Force area namely the O'Malley family headed by John Harry O'Malley and the Conway's headed by Patrick Conway. Intelligence suggests that the O'Malley family are taking possession of a large quantity of weapons, ammunition and explosives to utilise in this feud. Included in the arsenal are thought to be AK47's, rocket launchers and sniper rifles. The explosives are not commercially produced and have been put together by an independent bomb maker. They are obtaining this equipment from a criminal gang located in North Berwick, East Lothian, Scotland. They will be transporting these items by sea on a ship called Benjy's Boat and they will be used to cause carnage against the Conway's. They intend to kill hundreds of gangland rivals."

The intelligence was low grade but he now had something to corroborate his original report which had arrived from the Foreign Office. He had no idea how the Foreign Office had obtained their intelligence as they had refused to divulge the source. That would suggest it had come from an informant. He checked the intelligence sources details. Joey Carr was a low level criminal who probably would not be privy to info about importation or theft of serious weapons and explosives on this scale. More importantly he would be of no use to the Secret Service and unlikely to be the source of their intelligence. The provenance indicated he did not know the persons whom he overheard in the café talking about the weaponry. The intelligence sounded very suspect. He tried to obtain more info on Joey Carr's mobile number so he could interrogate his phone but nothing was listed. There was still nothing to go on. He ran a check on the café where the information had been overheard. The Romanian owner was on The Security Services files and he had some serious contacts that could possibly put a job like this together. The intelligence was still totally unconfirmed and there was nothing to suggest there was anything in it but the Romanian connection did give it some credence. Giles

Wainwright looked at the last piece of the report. PC Jamie Douglas was the originating officer. He logged into the personnel files of Northumbria Police. Jamie Douglas had a mobile phone number listed. He noted the number. Despite regulations forbidding them from doing so most police officers cultivating informants were tempted to maintain contact with their touts or snitches via unauthorised means. It was a fair bet that if Jamie Douglas intended to use Carr as an unofficial informant then he would have to contact him by phone. Douglas's phone would now have to be covertly monitored by the security services thought Giles Wainwright who needed to make sense of all this information. Some work had been done by the analysts who had obtained information on everything traceable from the original report. Details had been gathered about the County Hotel owners, their bank details, credit cards, DVLA records, phone records, website details, and any other details he could obtain from public or other searchable databases. He had looked at police reports, army records, family histories and scanned reams and reams of paper outlining every public aspect of the hotel, its guests and even it's suppliers but nothing obvious jumped out to suggest any link to terrorists. He summoned an analyst and told her to start documenting, collating and charting the information so that it may make sense. He gave her the new information about Joey Carr, PC Douglas, the O'Malleys, the Conways and the Romanian café owner and told her to find the intelligence that linked them all together with the County Hotel and Benjy's Boat in North Berwick. He also made arrangements for all vehicular traffic on the A1 between North Berwick and Newcastle to be monitored by means of an automatic number plate recognition system.

Sally was uncle Harry's favourite niece. She was one of many girls he had out working the pubs, clubs, streets and café's looking for useful information. She was part of his intelligence network. Information was a key factor in survival and Harry invested a lot in obtaining it. Sally's story of some drunk, amorous copper trying to worm his way into her knickers with tales of heroism and information on gangsters may or may not be useful but the bit about a large delivery of weaponry and explosives set off an alarm bell. He was aware of an enterprise to gain a similar consignment and this may or may not be connected but it would need to be checked out. He told Sally to team up with

Alicia, one of his high class girls, and to take the copper out for a good time as quickly as possible. Harry told Sally he would brief Alicia on her role. Sally started to make the necessary arrangements and Harry made a few calls to his associates. The name Joey Carr was passed on as a possible starting place.

Joseph Fallon and Michael O'Leary were briefed by the former IRA Quartermaster General. They were part of an Active Service Unit, a tight-knit cell isolated to improve security and operational capacity. They were well aware of the missing weapons cache as their cell had been given responsibility to search for its whereabouts almost as soon as the original cell that had hidden it was eliminated. Joseph Fallon had been involved in this task now for almost seven years. Michael O'Leary had joined the cell to replace one of its members who had disappeared never to be found but who was widely suspected of having been eliminated by the Security Services. The Quartermaster went over the normal security issues. No mobile phones, no communication with anyone out with the others presence; where possible avoid security cameras and CCTV. Avoid contact with the police and never let each other out of sight. If urgent communication was needed it would be done via coded messages to the designated cell phone of the day. He gave them each a coded list of numbers which he told them to memorize and destroy. The numbers were in a sequence which were easy to remember. He gave them three days to complete their mission and told them to be back by Sunday if possible. Other personnel could cover the auction and check out the buyers of the secluded property that was linked to the missing weapons cache. It would be weeks before any deeds changed hands or the buyers had access to the property. The Quartermaster would however try to speed things up in that respect if the bidding phase was successful. Fallon and O'Leary could be unleashed then if events in North Berwick didn't hold them up.

Giles Wainwright had acquired all the information he could without mounting a more pro-active operation. He had already flagged the intelligence as Security Services information and blocked other services including the police from accessing it. The suggestion the police could be compromised justified the exclusion of Lothian and

Borders or any other force from the information. He had registered the intelligence package under the name Operation Sigma and the man chosen to run the pro-active intelligence part of the operation was Alex McKenzie an experienced Scottish field operative, from Glasgow, with 20 years service. The strategy was decided. A surveillance team would be dispatched to North Berwick to follow up and seek out new leads surrounding the County Hotel. They would also try and discreetly obtain details of all ex-policemen residing in North Berwick and frequenting the County Hotel. An operation would be mounted in Tyneside to obtain CCTV evidence from the Romanian gangster's café and the surrounding areas to identify who Joey Carr had overheard in the next booth. Joey Carr would have to be discreetly interviewed. A Surveillance team would also shadow the Romanian gangster and the analyst would continue to receive and access information from the field and the other intelligence sources that developed. Operation Sigma moved into phase two.

Jamie Douglas had made it to work but he was hung over. He was sitting in the back of the local delicatessen forcing down a roll and sausage and a coffee supplied free by the proprietor who liked to stay on the right side of the local constabulary. The sausage was drowned in brown sauce and the coffee had four sugars. The proprietor looked at the policeman who was dressed in jeans, trainers and a bomber jacket. He was supposed to be undercover but the sound of his radio coupled with the baton, handcuffs and notebook which protruded from his pockets didn't do much for his disguise. The David Bowie song 'Life on Mars' and theme tune to top cop TV show 'Life on Mars' began to play inside the officers jacket. Jamie Douglas began searching for his phone and in doing so neglected his attention to the sausage roll. As brown sauce dripped all over his jeans he took Sally's call. *"Yes he could be free that afternoon"* he confirmed. Making the necessary arrangements and ending the call, he announced that his efforts last night had not been in vain as the bird he had pulled at the club had the hots for him and she was gagging for it. He thought about how to slope off early to ensure she wasn't disappointed.

Uncle Harry was of Turkish decent hence his rather crude nickname Harry 'the Turk' which no one used to his face. Harry was proud of his Turkish culture but would not take kindly to being called 'Turk' and he had already caused the death or disfigurement of a number of disrespectful associates who had neglected this dislike. Harry was a key figure in a well connected global criminal consortium and he had the power of life or death over the majority of people he met. This power required respect, money, weapons and contacts. He had more than sufficient amounts in all these aspects but one could never have enough of any of them and a business opportunity had arisen in Dublin which although no great secret in the world of global crime was proving elusive to all those involved in the game. A number of his associates were already heading to Dublin to further his organisation's aims but could it be possible that a rival faction had somehow got ahead of the rest. The IRA had been very careful by keeping knowledge of their arsenal's location to only four people. This proved disastrous when they took the secret to their graves. The IRA suspected the Security Services of foul play but the British Government had not claimed the publicity and acclaim they would normally credit themselves with if a major weapon haul was seized. Arguably this could have been deliberate to avoid derailing the peace talks but Harry considered that an unlikely prospect. The Security Services, the IRA, the Russians, the Chinese and even Al Qaida were crawling about the banks and hills surrounding the Irish lake where the cache had been hidden so Harry believed it was still a prize waiting to be found. Firepower was a defining matter in any argument and the firm that recovered this particular arsenal would seriously increase their chances in any skirmish with their rivals, so it was sought after by them all. There was also the other matter, the matter of a bigger prize which could be sold to the highest bidder. Harry made arrangements to meet one of his associates and to put the necessary wheels in motion just in case someone in North Berwick was ahead of the rest of the chasing pack.

The small unobtrusive man who had left Kurdistan was now within Atatürk Airport in Istanbul waiting for a flight to Frankfurt which was the next leg of his journey on his way to Dublin. His three associates were still with him. Bilal his personal assistant was checking in their baggage. The two bodyguards were busy being vigilant. Everything was going to plan.

Rupert Basingstoke had firmly but tactfully managed to persuade his niece not to bother him anymore. He obliterated all thoughts of North Berwick terrorists and turned his attention to Operation Chameleon which targeted information and technology obtained by the Russians and Chinese, vital information which could upset the balance of military power in favour of the East. This Operation spanned the globe and he had numerous Secret Service operatives in various parts of the world feeding him intelligence and actively infiltrating and stealing or sabotaging the work and technology of the various enemies or rivals of the UK. He could see the comparison between himself and the movie character M who had a number of secret agents, including 007 or James Bond who were licensed to kill but the reality was M was a figurehead whilst he was the driving force behind his secret organisation. It was he who had the licence to kill and his agents were merely his weapons of choice. He was accountable for every action of his service and many of the countries Special Forces. He had plans to utilise them in taking out or eliminating a few of the enemies in Operation Chameleon but he was not yet in a position to determine who, when or why he would do so. That would be decided by the information provided by his undercover operatives in the shady world of international espionage.

Alex McKenzie was a methodical, efficient and careful operator as most good intelligence operatives were. He had drawn up the necessary intelligence packages and issued them to the various teams which he had chosen to undertake them. The surveillance team was now in place taking observations on the South Shields Romanian café. A number of frauds had been identified in the area and specialist operatives had presented themselves at nearby premises posing as the Regional Crime Squad investigating these crimes. They had quickly obtained all the relevant CCTV footage which could possibly show the persons who had been in the booth adjacent to Carr entering or leaving the premises. Analysts were already scrutinising them. Covert surveillance cameras were quickly set up in the area to cover the café and these were being monitored. Plans were made to break into the café premises that night and ensure every table was bugged and covert cameras were placed to identify who was talking. A team was sent to locate and identify Joey Carr who was appearing at the local Crown Court.

Giles Wainright kept himself up to date with everything that was happening. He had now set up a control room and his analysts and staff were constantly updated about everything happening in the field. *"What's happening in North Berwick?"* He asked. *"Nothing much yet"* came the reply. *"There is only one security camera in the whole town and it doesn't view the County Hotel. We've got the footage from last Sunday but we're struggling to identify anyone of note."* Giles was updated regarding enquiries on ex-policemen. The covert interrogation of the Lothian and Borders personnel files had revealed several, most of which were ex-senior officers. An enquiry conducted with some deceit at the local office by a security service agent posing as reporter for the local paper, looking for a story on successful ex-North Berwick police officers, was told by the station officer that one of the local taxi companies, Jim's Cabs, was run by a retired officer George Logan. Giles found nothing untoward in George Logan's files that would merit any kind of attention but on hearing of the nature of Logan's new occupation Alex McKenzie, well versed in the connections between taxi owners in his native Glasgow and organised crime, highlighted him as a likely candidate for further surveillance. Covert cameras were also installed covering the front and rear of the County Hotel. One of these was concealed in a light on the building opposite the front of the hotel. Plans were also being made to bug the hotel. One of the first vehicles to arrive on the scene was a taxi owned by Jim's Cabs and driven by George Logan. Ian Steel saw George's cab and went out to talk to him about advance bookings. This conversation between taxi company owner and hotel owner put them firmly on the analyst's charts as associates and tracking devices were later placed on all George's cars. The tactics and equipment of the security services were now being deployed and utilised in Operation Sigma.

Joseph Fallon and Michael O'Leary left Eire and travelled across the border into Northern Ireland then onto Larne. It was not the most comfortable journey they had undertaken as they were secreted in specially concealed compartments within large lorries. This was necessary to avoid custom checks or police attention which might alert the authorities to their presence. Following a reasonably calm ferry crossing their respective vehicles dropped them of in the Scottish town of Stranraer where they met at a silver BMW motor vehicle which had been left specifically for their use. Joseph Fallon was a heavy set man. He was now in his early forties but he still had a thick mop of dark hair and a pronounced Southern Irish accent. He had distinct circular scarring on the right side of his neck which he had sustained during a pub brawl when his assailant had gouged a broken bottle into him. He liked to tell people he had been hit by a bullet fired by a British paratrooper but anyone with any knowledge of bullet wounds or scarring would know instantly this was not the case. He had been disfigured in a bar room brawl when he challenged a suspected British soldier. He had pulled up a stranger in a Republican bar but a bottle smashed across the side of his head had dazed him, and then the sharp end stabbed and twisted into his neck had maimed him. His assailant was never seen again and all attempts to identify and kill the stranger had eluded him but Joseph Fallon still bore the grudge and had the face of his attacker firmly etched in his mind. None of the IRA intelligence or contacts could identify the soldier but Fallon just knew he was army, SAS, Special Branch or a policeman. Logan had a good description of the bastard but no army, police or intelligence unit personnel matched the description. Everyone who knew Fallon knew he considered this unfinished business. Fallon turned to Michael O'Leary and told him to drive. Fallon didn't dislike O'Leary but there was something about the upstart that irritated him. O'Leary talked too much. He was full of bravado about what he could do but in truth he had done nothing. O'Leary had done well in all the training. He could shoot targets, he could fight on the training ground and had even roughed up a couple of heavies when playing enforcer in the field but he had never really done anything that could count as real action. He had never used a sniper rifle on a British patrol or set off an explosive device in a roadside ambush. As far as Fallon was concerned O'Leary was still green. He was smart and quick witted but no one knew how clever or calm they really were until they experienced the need to act in the field. O'Leary had been seconded to the active service unit after the cease fire so he had never really had the chance to prove himself. He was not true IRA, he was an outsider. He was a mercenary fighting someone else's war but he talked like he had hated the Brits all his life. They had killed his friend and that's why he joined the cause. The Quartermaster had stated clearly that O'Leary was to become part of the team as he represented the faction who had supplied the knowledge that allowed the concealment of the cache. Fallon knew O'Leary was not even the bastard's real name, in fact he doubted the bastard was even Irish. That irked Fallon but he still couldn't help liking the young twat. O'Leary had just turned thirty years of age. He was tall, slim, fair and handsome. He had a smile that would melt ice and a manner that made him instantly likeable to both men and women alike. Men wanted to enter his circle of friends and women wanted to enter his bed. No big ugly scars on O'Leary, plenty of women for him. Fallon was slightly envious of that. The only women he got now were the ones he took. The ones he knew would submit to his will without a formal complaint either through fear or some respect for his position in the movement and his dedication to the cause. Most women he thought were put off by the scar. One day some bastard would pay for the scar but meanwhile O'Leary would pay. *"Right you little gobshite how long to North Berwick?"* Fallon smiled.

"Four hours ya bog dwelling bastard, if you'd went to school like I did you would know these things. Did you check the boot?" O'Leary asked.

"Aye the Russians are in the back", replied Fallon.

And so two Irishmen travelled in a German BMW,

with two Russian-manufactured Makarov PB suppressed pistols in the boot, and drove to the Scottish town of North Berwick.

Jamie Douglas had escaped from work. He had ditched his police radio, notebook and baton along with his stab proof vest and CS gas canister in his locker at work along with his other equipment but he still had his handcuffs. He reckoned Sally was a right little police groupie and if he played his cards right he might have her in handcuffs later. He was to meet her at three o'clock at Rosie Malone's in Market Place, South Shields. He knew the pub and he arrived on time. He looked about. There was no sign of Sally yet so he ordered a pint of Marston's Pedigree. He grabbed the pint tumbler and stuck it to his mouth. He swallowed down the premium beer and turned to the doorway where the sight of Sally almost made him choke on his pint. He recovered quickly and composed himself. He saw her recognise him and walk towards him. *'Oh God, he had been drunk last night,'* he thought. Sally was no looker. She was small and dumpy. On the plus side she was blonde and had an exceptional pair of tits but her legs were a little heavy and she was dressed like a tent in an orange dress with black spangle flecked tights and gold high heeled shoes. She flashed a smile at him which showed her white but uneven teeth. He didn't feel so good about this date now and he hoped no one in the pub would recognise him.

Sally put her arm round him and winked *"I'll have a Coke big boy"* she whispered and pecked him on the cheek.

Jamie ordered the Coke, ignoring the smug look the barman gave him. Did he think she was his lass? *"You want ice?"*, Jamie asked trying to reemphasise the fact he didn't really know her.

"Can't you remember? You bought me enough last night" Sally teased.

The barman gave another smug look and Jamie couldn't really remember last night but he acted decisively *"Ice and Lemon"* he said.

"See you do remember" Sally said and pecked Jamie on the cheek again.

Jamie immediately regretted his decisiveness but decided, against his instincts, not to do a runner immediately. If he could get this fat lass out of here quickly he could go to a quiet pub where there was less chance of anyone knowing him and he would seek an opportunity to get his wicked way with her before dumping her. He couldn't have the lads at work finding out about this conquest but *'Your hole's your hole and fat lasses need love too'* he thought, feeling the handcuffs nestled in his jacket pocket.

Sally interrupted his thoughts. *"I hope you don't mind but I told my friend Alicia that I was meeting you here. She might pop in for a quick visit. She was very jealous when I said I was meeting a policeman."* She pecked him on the cheek again.

Jamie had mixed emotions. Two fat groupies were worse than one but if he could bed them both at once then it might well be a conquest to boast about.

"Here she is now" exclaimed Sally excitedly.

Jamie turned and just couldn't believe his eyes. Alicia was a beauty. Her figure was outstanding and she had a smile to die for. Jamie hadn't really ever believed in love, never mind love at first sight, but he was spellbound and captivated by the alluring, beautiful and smiling, at him, Alicia.

Harry 'the Turk' had already briefed Alicia on what he expected and wanted from Jamie

Douglas. She was to milk him dry of any information that could be gleaned about the weaponry and who was sourcing it. She would use her talents, of which she had many, how and when she saw fit but use them she would and sooner rather than later. Harry had three further appointments to deal with that afternoon. One related to travel arrangements. Another involved briefing three of his henchmen about their proposed trip to North Berwick and the final one was a meeting with a Romanian acquaintance Serghei. He was looking forward to a decent cup of Turkish coffee which he always obtained from his associate's Romanian Coffee shop. He entered the shop and was greeted immediately by Serghei who was expecting and waiting for him. "*Salut*" beamed Serghei looking very respectful and pleased to see his guest. There was no other way to greet Harry unless you wanted to incur his wrath and that normally wasn't a clever thing to do.

"*Ah Sergei bey*" retorted Harry and both men warmly shook hands. The meeting went well, very well apart from one slight moment of confusion where one of Serghei's employees switched on too many appliances in the kitchen and tripped the mains switch. The loss of electrical power plunged the place into complete darkness and Harry couldn't see two inches in front of his face. The blackout blinds were very effective even during the day. Harry had considered shooting someone but he couldn't see anyone to shoot. The circuit breaker was quickly restored before anyone killed anyone and Serghei apologised profusely for the interruption. The kitchen worker had to leave the kitchen area for hygiene reasons as blood near food was not a good policy but once the light was restored everyone settled down and got back to business.

In a covert monitoring post some miles away two secret servicemen watched this exchange on their video monitor and tried to listen to the conversation. The blackout disrupted their visual imaging but the audio failed when Serghei and Harry took their conversation into the kitchen which was an area the technical team had not thought to bug. The video pictures were analysed and the surveillance photos taken when Harry had entered the café were downloaded for identification purposes. Alex McKenzie was subsequently made aware of Harry 'the Turk' becoming involved in the enquiry and he authorised another surveillance team being placed on him. This was becoming a very manpower intensive operation and surveillance operatives were becoming thin on the ground.

Benjamin Black had been summoned. He had a splitting headache and felt like shit. He was now 43 years old and didn't have much to show for himself and if the truth be told he also hated himself. Running his fingers though his thick black hair he massaged the birthmark that formed a patch around his right eye and tried to focus his mind on why at this particular moment in time Harry 'the Turk' wanted to see him urgently. '*Had he fucked up again*?' Harry didn't take kindly to fuck ups and as arrogant and abusive as Ben may be, he knew better than to be arrogant and abusive in front of Harry. Ben was six foot two and skinny as a rake. This was nothing to do with healthy eating. He knew he didn't eat well and he smoked far too much. The continued abuse of spirits and cocaine helped to ease the tension and depression he felt about his position in life but drunk or sober he was close to suicidal. Not quite there yet but close. He didn't have the guts for suicide it was too final and fear of Harry often kept his mind fixed on the little errands and rewards he obtained by doing

Harry's dirty work. Everything he owned was Harry's. Ben hadn't had a proper job for over ten years but then again he had never, ever had a proper job. The birthmark around his right eye had made him insecure for as long as he could remember. Panda face, patch, black eye, Dalmatian face were some of the less insulting taunts he had endured but he literally had a face like a well skelped arse and he didn't feel too comfortable with that. The Navy had been his first career but he got out of that after 6 years. A short spell in the Metropolitan Police followed before his involvement with drugs forced him to resign. Harry 'the Turk' had taken him under his wing then and black eyed Benji had been Harry's mule moving drugs, woman and contraband wherever and when ever Harry wanted. Harry wanted him now and that meant he would have to shake off the shitty feeling, smarten himself up and see Harry soon because to piss off Harry was one sure way to meet a certain death far more painful than any suicide attempt could ever be. Ben washed, put on a clean shirt and climbed the stairs onto the boat deck. He surveyed the St Peter's Marina which had around 150 pontoon berths all with electricity and water. The marina was located on the river just a mile from Newcastle city centre. Many people would consider living on a yacht in a luxury marina an ideal lifestyle but it was worse than living in a caravan. The yacht belonged to Harry and Ben had no claim on it at all. In truth Ben belonged to Harry too and as far as Ben could see that would never change. Ben owed Harry more money than he could ever earn and the only way he could earn was working for Harry who had him securely by the balls. Ben often thought of disappearing with the yacht and some of Harry's drugs but that would be a silly thing to do. Harry's influence was global and Harry would find him and deal with him in an unpleasant manner when he did. There was nothing for it but to do what Harry wished. He jumped from the yacht and walked to the excellent and busy bar and restaurant the "Bascule" which was located within the marina.

Malky stood at the top of Berwick Law, an extinct volcano, with its panoramic views of East Lothian and beyond. To the west he could see Edinburgh Castle and the Forth Bridge. To the north he could see the Firth of Forth and Fife coastline and to the east he could see the ancient curtain walls of Tantallon Castle and the Lammermuir Hills were visible to the south. He had just walked his dog, Max, from the car park at the foot of Berwick Law and he had followed the track round the base of the Law for a short distance before starting the ascent. He had climbed the path on the south west on to a plateau over a former quarry and then continued on the winding path to the summit, 615 feet above sea level. His legs were aching, his chest was heaving and he just knew he was unfit. He was no stranger to the Law, He climbed it at least once every two months but it was getting harder. One year of "easy life" had taken its toll. Too much drink, too much food, too many hours stuck in front of a computer and not enough exercise had left him carrying an extra couple of stone and he knew he really had to do something about it. The old Clash song 'I fought the law and the law won' suddenly took on new meaning. As a policeman he taken meaning from all sorts of songs and applied them to the job. Whistling the Clash had been a good way to escort a ned to the cells but now the song was starting to signify something else. 'I fought the law and the law won' now meant he was a fat bastard.

Over the centuries the North Berwick Law had been used as a look out post to warn of approaching enemies. It was told that a nun lit a beacon on the summit in 1544 when English ships entered the Firth of Forth. The stone building at the summit was erected in 1803 as a signal station during the Napoleonic Wars. Lieutenant Leyden was in command with a party of Naval Ratings who were instructed to light a beacon on the sight of enemy forces which would then start a chain of fires on high points across the country, providing an early warning system. There was also a concrete observation post used during World War 1 and World War 2. Now the Law was warning Malky of the impending invasion of a fat ass and a growing gut. He made a decision to eat less junk food, consume more fruit and vegetables and start a proper exercise programme. Looking out once more at the stunning view of North Berwick he started his descent walking past the whale jaw bone that has been present at the top of Berwick Law since 1709 as a land mark to guide the sailors home safely. The latest new 5m high whale bone was made from fibreglass and had been lifted into position by helicopter on 26th June 2008. Malky hoped to get to the bottom without the aid of a helicopter and decided it was time to head for the County. Nothing in his new fitness regime made any reference to giving up alcohol and he could already visualise the pint sitting on the bar. *"Right Max come on we're going for a pint"*, he announced. It was good to have a plan.

Malky wasn't the only one heading for the High Street. The two Irishmen Joseph Fallon and Michael O'Leary had been given the address of a holiday flat which had been sourced from one of the local letting agents at short notice. The flat had its own allocated parking bay and the keys were to be uplifted from the letting office in the High Street. Micheal O'Leary who was not as obviously Irish as Joseph Fallon was, picked up the keys and settled the account in cash. They then made their way to a beachside location on the east side of town which offered superb views of the sea. Joseph Fallon was not unhappy with his current task but he was not enamoured by it either. He knew the importance of intelligence gathering but considered this a menial task which was a waste of his talents. He had spent the last few years trying to ascertain how two container loads of weapons could mysteriously disappear off the face of the earth. O'Leary and his smart ass associates were responsible and now his smart ass associates were putting pressure on the IRA to ensure no one else found the cache. Fallon still thought O'Leary couldn't really be trusted but he had now been working with the snotty free stater for over 4 years now and had to admit he was alright for an orange bastard which was how Fallon saw everyone who wasn't a hundred percent Irish and committed to the cause. Three days at the sea side might be fun he thought, '*Ah hope the Guinness is good*'. They went to the Auld Hoose pub and found that it was. They sat inconspicuously by the open fire in pleasant surroundings and listened whilst they enjoyed a very nice pint or two. They heard absolutely nothing that suggested anyone in the pub knew anything about weapons.

The Marston's Pedigree was good and Jamie Douglas just couldn't help himself. He had been besotted by the gorgeous Alicia and much to his relief wee fat Sally had disappeared. Alicia appeared genuinely interested in him, his work and his body and Jamie was certainly interested in her body but something else was at work here. It wasn't just lust, he wanted to impress her. She was the woman of his dreams, he was in love. She was knowledgeable about the Newcastle underworld too. Jamie had tried to impress her with his exploits in the job but she knew people from the Regional Crime Squads and the Met. She knew all the gangland figures and without actually telling him anything alluded to what was happening on the streets. Jamie started to exaggerate his knowledge and made up a few things that he thought would please her. She told him she liked him and gave him her number. He was to call her and she would see him tomorrow. Jamie watched her slender figure as she glided to the door. She turned, blew him a kiss and disappeared. Jamie was infatuated by her. He had to improve his game if he was going to keep her interested. He headed back to his office where he logged on to the intelligence system and began to learn a few things about the Newcastle underworld. He needed information if he was to keep his chances alive with the beautiful, captivating and seductive Alicia. He considered what he was doing. He was interrogating police systems for reasons other than police work and that was a serious breach of regulations but Jamie decided he could justify his interest because he needed to research what Joey Carr had told him. He pondered his next move. Police systems were audited and it would be obvious to the administrators what he was looking at and who he was checking on. He decided he would have to play clever. As long as he was submitting intelligence he would be justified in researching it but he couldn't just submit intelligence without a credible source. He considered his options. Joey Carr was the obvious choice but he had already used him and hadn't been in contact with him since. He had picked up a few bits and pieces from Alicia but he didn't want to insert the new love of his life's name into the police intelligence system. '*Fat Sally*', he mused. He had her contact details and she was sort of there when he spoke to Alicia so he would make up a few juicy snippets based loosely on what Alicia had said and use fat Sally as the source. He set to work composing another intelligence report.

Benjy was sitting in his usual place beside the coal fire in the bar of the County Hotel, supping a nice pint of Guinness. He was sporting a dark blue woollen Arran style jumper with a zipper at the front. It looked like a traditional fisherman's jumper. Malky who had successfully navigated his way from the top of the Berwick Law turned to Bradley, *"Have you got yourself a Benjy jumper for the Somalia trip yet*?", he chortled.

"Fuck off" said Bradley *"I'm wearing me Magpies top"*

"You don't have a fuckin Newcastle top and it's a well known fact the ladies like a sailor so you'll need a Benjy Jumper" challenged Malky.

"Hey Nina would you prefer a man in a fisherman's jumper or a football top?", asked Bradley.

"How much money is in their wallets?", retorted Nina.

"Shut it witch" retorted Bradley.

"Are You taking to me?" asked Sioban who had just entered the bar along with Carol and Sheila. North Berwick was famous for its witch trials as in 1590 a number of people from East Lothian were accused of witchcraft by King James VI who prosecuted them for holding their covens on the Auld Kirk Green, part of the modern day harbour area, and cavorting with the devil and evil spirits. The County Hotels three witches were certainly renowned for their association with spirits. They met every Wednesday night under the guise of 'the Skinny/Fat Club.' Their aim was to avoid the local slimming club fee by weighing themselves and saving money for their holidays. With the number of spirits they conjured up in the bar it was hard to see how any savings were made. Lorraine joined them to make up the holiday quartet and the

spirits began to appear at their table. King James would have had them all burned and the whisky and rum they consumed would certainly have provided the necessary accelerants.

Two strangers walked into the bar as the giggling subsided. One ordered a Guinness and a vodka and Coke for his companion. Malky and Bradley returned to their conversation and the two strangers sat at a table. Pablo was drunk. He wasn't working today and he had some free time to pursue his favourite hobbies which were lager or Jack Daniels and Coke. Today he indulged with great gusto. He stared through one eye at the latest additions to the clientele. *'Hmm I'm going to keep an eye on you,'* he thought.

Alex McKenzie had not been able to obtain the relevant authorisation to bug the County Hotel. The Romanian café in South Shields was owned by people of dubious character so that had been relatively easy to authorise under English law. Placing trackers on cars or cameras in public places was also easy but to break into and bug a property owned by law abiding citizens and freely accessible to the public in Scotland was not quite as acceptable to the Scottish courts and even the security services had to play by the rules sometimes. Alex McKenzie liked to think he could overcome any logistical or bureaucratic problems and that was part of the reason he was given certain jobs in the first place. The legal people, in Scotland, however were not impressed with his arguments and for that reason he had to resort to more old fashioned methods. As a result he had to send two operatives into the County Hotel to eavesdrop on as many conversations as they could. They had been given a list of key words to listen for as well as obvious conversations about weaponry and criminality. 'Benjy's boat' was one such item on the list.

Emma Ferguson was enjoying her vodka and Coke. The atmosphere within the pub was very friendly and the clientele were in high spirits. Humorous banter was being exchanged by various customers and it was obvious outsiders were made welcome. The barmaid was friendly and polite. The punters although loud were courteous to strangers, if not to each other, and several remarks or apologies had been made in her general direction which would have allowed her to join in the conversations had she wished. The crowd sitting around the tables appeared to have just finished their work and were unwinding. A few guys were standing around the bar and one was sitting at the jukebox giving her a funny look. She decided it wasn't a threatening look or a dangerous look but more of an admiring look. At 35 years old with a slim figure, blonde hair and relatively large breasts she was certainly aware what an admiring look was like. The gentleman concerned was on first impression relatively good looking too. Emma whispered in her companion's ear and stood. She made her way towards the gentleman. *"Which way are the toilets?"* She asked.

Pablo had been temporarily distracted by a commotion at the bar. Max 'the Westie' had ventured to the bar in an effort to explore the anal regions of a fellow canine who was lying beneath his masters stool. The resultant growl that greeted Max caused his quick retreat as he scurried back to the safety of the tables. Malky chastised his dog for being a wimp as his tormentor was half the size of him. Colin the local 'Scouser' who was fed up trying to convince every one he wasn't a 'Scouser', because he was from the Wirral, looked up from his paper. *"My money's on Brillo"* He announced.

Emma Thomson looked down at what looked like a pot scrubber on legs with a growl like a grizzly bear. *'Animal lovers couldn't be terrorists'* she thought, applying typical British psyche to her assessment of the clientele.

Pablo looked up and realised the latest love of his life was now talking to him. *'I've been watching you, giving you the eye and you've responded,'* he thought. He smiled showing the absence of a front tooth and the stump where the crown should have been fixed to. He directed her to the ladies toilet. *"Through the glass door and along the corridor to the left"*, he slurred, leaning over to point the way.

Emma Ferguson thanked him and headed for the loo. He had been a big disappointment, too drunk to chew his fingernails and no teeth to do it with. It was a pity because she thought he had seemed cute before he opened his mouth. Emma took care of her toiletry needs and returned to her table. One or two friendly remarks again enticed her into a conversation with a few of the locals. She finished her drink and left along with her companion with thank you and good byes echoing in her ears. *"We'll that didn't seem like a terrorist pub"* said Emma to her companion when she was out of earshot. *"I think we should go back."*

Surveillance operations in pubs followed various guidelines. They had only been in the pub to gain a quick reconnoitre of the interior and its customers. When she was debriefed she was going to suggest that her companion and her continued to visit instead of sending in various different units on a rotational basis. The customers had been so friendly that she foresaw no problems in establishing a rapport with them that would allow her to gauge the intentions of the patrons and identify any potential terrorists. So far the only information she had gleaned was that some guy Stevie Duncan was possibly signing for the darts team.

Joey Carr had been released from South Shields County Court but he was still a prisoner. He now had no idea where he was. He was blindfolded and tied to a chair. He had felt what he thought was a baseball bat or rounded piece of wood being rolled carefully along the side of his head and then he heard the swish and an almighty thud as the bat smashed against a wall close to his head. This process had been repeated several times over the course of maybe four hours. He reckoned there were three other people in the place with him but no one spoke. He pleaded to be let go. He demanded to be freed but no one uttered a word.

They just laughed. Joey was sobbing, he had pissed himself and he was terrified but he had no idea why he was strapped to the chair.

Alex McKenzie reflected on the day's work. He had covered every base he could think of and the plot was thickening. There had been no video systems in the Romanian café but all the CCTV he could find had been seized from the vicinity of the location. That was now being looked at by analysts. They had identified Jamie Carr entering and leaving the café. The only person of any interest who had been identified entering or leaving around the same time was a local drug dealer. His file was being pulled and the analysts would work on that too. The other patrons had looked like students, businessmen, pensioners and women out for a coffee. The historic CCTV footage hadn't taken them anywhere. The live operation had identified Harry 'the Turk' as an associate of Serghei the Romanian café owner and that proved interesting. It might have been more interesting if the techies had bugged the kitchen too. All was not lost though because the subsequent surveillance on 'the Turk' had taken his team to the St Peter's Marina in Newcastle where they had seen 'the Turk' meet with three males. Following a meeting in the Bascule Restaurant, the three males boarded a yacht and appeared to be making it seaworthy. The yacht was called the Delta Queen and it was owned by Harry 'the Turk'. A static surveillance unit was watching the yacht and Harry was still being tailed. He would need more resources and would have to make plans if the yacht moved. His boss, Giles Wainwright, would have to sort that out.

North Berwick hadn't really produced anything of note. The historic CCTV had drawn a complete blank. The live operation had been impeded because of bureaucracy and he had to utilise even more resources to watch the County Hotel. All his surveillance personnel now wanted the job. The squads had already started joking about the pub surveillance rosters being dish washing or pot scrubbing duties because the most aggressive thing they'd come across in there was a four legged dish scourer with a snarl like a wolf. The County, it seemed was a cracking little hotel where everyone was friendly and the patter was brilliant. His staff were being welcomed by the punters and even invited back. This was no normal surveillance job and McKenzie didn't like it. Had his men been rumbled already or was it just a really friendly pub? He had no choice. The operation would have to continue until Giles Wainwright told him otherwise. He would continue to rotate personnel into the pub as and when the covert surveillance post observed persons of interest going in. He checked his watch. It was 11.30pm. The logs showed the only persons within were the manager, his wife, the barmaid and most of the residents. The residents check had found nothing of note but one of the guests appeared to be a Geordie. Bradley Bone's file was being pulled. The analysts would be working on it shortly. George Logan the ex-policeman taxi driver had just left the pub along with Scott Hunter, the roofer. That provided another link between the ex-policeman and the hotel but a taxi-driver picking up a hire was not exactly an act of international terrorism. North Berwick had yielded absolutely nothing but operations like this could take time. The Newcastle work had begun to show dividends already and that was a bonus. He suddenly remembered Joey Carr. He made a note to check on the team who had been tasked to find and interrogate him.

5 - THURSDAY

Giles Wainwright was in early as usual and was on his second cup of coffee. He had looked through the items in his in tray and he was now checking the latest e-mail messages in his inbox to bring himself up to date with any events that had taken place since he had left the previous evening. The Operation Sigma control room was busy and analysts were working away on the various data streams that were flowing into the system. Whilst some of the events which were beginning to unfold looked interesting nothing really concrete had developed and that worried him. He now had a control room in place, three observation stations, a host of technical surveillance and several surveillance teams deployed in both Newcastle and North Berwick. The cost of the operation was escalating and he was now looking for a naval station, a radar unit or a reconnaissance plane to be put on standby in case they had to monitor the activities of a motor cruiser which was expected to put to sea shortly. He looked at the photographs of the people Harry 'the Turk' had met at the marina. They were mean looking brutes and one had distinctive markings around his eye which should make him easy to identify. His phone rang. The boat was on the move. *"Someone get that boat tagged I want to know where it goes"*, he Shouted. Someone replied *"Right sir"* and he knew the task would be accomplished.

Benjamin Black wasn't particularly impressed by his two new crew members but he was used to dealing with their type. They had been dumped on him by Harry 'the Turk' and his instructions were to take them to North Berwick where Harry had sorted out a mooring for him. At 35 feet long his boat was approaching the maximum size for the small North Berwick harbour but Harry assured him he could anchor or moor his boat in the West Bay. All the permanent moorings there were private, except for the three most easterly moorings, which were owned by East Lothian Yacht Club, and they were primarily over tide moorings, but they could be used for overnight stops by visiting yachts, affiliated to an RYA recognised club, for a small fee. Harry was a member of every club that was worth being a member of and he had already taken care of the small fee. All Benjamin had to do was get his crew there, drop them off to snoop about and then bring them back and report their findings to Harry. The weather forecast was fine for the next few days, after the recent big storm, and it was a relatively short trip for his motor cruiser. The journey was about a hundred nautical miles. Once he hit the open sea he could do that in 5 hours at a steady 20 knots. He could even knock an hour or so off if he opened up the throttle to get the 30 knots of speed that the cruiser was capable of, but first he still had 7 miles of the Tyne to navigate and with a 6 knot speed limit curtailing his progress that meant an hour to the open sea.

Joey Carr was cold and confused. He was sitting in a pool of his own urine and his trousers were soaking. The people who had kidnapped him had stopped hitting the wall by his head but they were still in the room. A chair was dragged along the floor and he sensed someone sit down next to him. He heard a rustle of cellophane like a cigarette packet being opened and this was followed by the noise of a lighter clicking. His new companion inhaled and exhaled as a cigarette was lit and the smell of cigarette smoke was a welcome distraction from the stench of his own piss. *"What do you want?"* Joey stammered. He was now worried about the prospect of cigarette burns being inflicted on him. If the baseball bat they had earlier threatened him was wielded at his head with the same force as it had hit the wall it would be a quick end. Cigarette burns would be painful and numerous but then again so could blows with the bat to his arms, legs, hands, feet, fingers, toes or body. He felt an urge to piss again but managed to control it.

"We want a little information" stated a foreign sounding voice.

"Anything, just ask" Joey spluttered.

"You have some information about guns and explosives, yes?", asked his interrogator.

Jamie hesitated. Were these guys going to kill him for being a grass? He had told the police some shit he had overheard in a café and now he was going to die for it. He felt the baseball bat rest on his knee and he panicked. His mind was too confused to bluff or to play smart. He couldn't think about who had captured him or how to play along to gain an advantage so he just blabbed. *"I don't really know anything ah just heard some blokes discussing stuff in a café. I made up most of the stuff I told the police just to get out but the bastards still locked me up. Honest I don't know anything."*

Joey's interrogator was patient and skilful. He quickly ascertained the location of the café in which the information had been overheard in. Joey told him the names O'Malley and Conway had been suggested by the police but they had never actually been heard in the conversation. Somali were the name he had heard and Benjy's boat had something to do with it. Joey's recollection of events was distorted but he put the whole thing into some kind of order to please his interrogator and hopefully save his life. A team of Somalis had contacts in North Berwick and they were planning a big hit job in Tyneside. They planned to kill rivals. They had bomb makers, AK47s, snipers rifles and it was all being brought to Newcastle in Benjy's boat next week. He knew all this because he overheard the conversation in the café. Yes he knew of the Romanian guy who owned the café. Yes it might have been him whom he overheard. No! He wasn't sure. No! He wasn't trying to protect him. OK it probably was him. Yes it was the café owner. Joey now had a shattered knee. Two fractured ribs and three teeth missing. He was spitting blood and saying what he thought would save his life. As soon as he mentioned Somalis his interrogator had become interested in the café owner. The interrogator didn't particularly like the café owner and any opportunity to undermine him had to be exploited. This wasn't a very professional attitude but the interrogator now had a hidden agenda. Joey's initial reluctance to expand on the café owner's involvement had led to violence being inflicted upon him and he now said anything that he thought would stop the baseball bat being wielded against him. When the interrogation was over the interrogator reckoned he had something to tell his boss. The main problem now was where to kill Joey Carr. Do they do it here or keep him alive until they reach his final resting place? Smashing his knee cap had been effective but that now meant he couldn't walk so he would have to be carried to his grave anyway. Maybe they should kill him here? He would ask the boss.

Alex McKenzie was not a happy man. Joey
Carr was now a problem. His men had been too
late arriving at the court and they had missed him.
The little shit had disappeared off the face of the
planet and the security services couldn't find him.
He left the team leader in no doubt about their
failings and told him to sort it. Joey Carr had to be
interviewed to find out what he did or did not
know, that was a significant line of enquiry that he
could not afford to overlook.

Charlie Brandon was at his desk in the
Northumbrian Police Divisional Intelligence Office
when he came across another intelligence report
submitted by PC Jamie Douglas. It was all vague
stuff about The O'Malleys and the Conways. The
report suggested they were big players moving a
lot of drugs but there was no real actionable
intelligence. Charlie looked at the provenance of
the intelligence and saw it was sourced from Sally
Demir. Strange name he thought and he decided to
do some research.

Harry 'the Turk' was perplexed, paranoid
and a little apprehensive. He was not afraid of

anyone but he was terrified of being outsmarted or losing the respect of his rivals. Every one was a potential enemy in his game, even allies and business partners. The reality was Harry could trust no one. He mused over the events of the past forty eight hours. His interest had been sparked by events unfolding in Dublin. A number of his competitors were interested in a property auction which it was rumoured was really a ruse for an arms deal. Harry had heard that even the ruse was a subterfuge and that some sort of secret weapon was actually up for grabs. The idea that his rivals were competing to obtain something that could leave him at a disadvantage irked him. Then the rather unsubstantiated news about a team in North Berwick supplying guns and explosives had reached his ears. It was probably nothing to do with Dublin but there was a Tyneside connection and it didn't do any harm checking these things out. He had contacted his associate Serghei, the Romanian as they both had an interest in the Dublin developments and they arranged a little joint venture to check out the North Berwick angle. Serghei had supplied two of his operatives to scout the area and Harry had supplied a boat and a captain to get them there. Now there was a suggestion that Serghei was involved in some kind of double cross and Harry could be the intended target. His interrogator told him about the involvement of Somalis. Sergei was well connected with the Somalis. Muslim Somalis were the latest gangsters that the UK had opened its door to. Somali gangs were now plying their trade across Britain. They had established themselves in North London where they openly dealt rocks of class-A drugs. Somali gangs were selling what they call 'Euro drugs' to the students and holidaymakers who streamed off the Eurostar link with the continent at King's Cross. Harry thought there were probably as many as a quarter of a million Somali immigrants in the UK and most of them were illegal. Somali gangs were major players in the trade of illegal drugs in Britain's big cities and they had become ruthless money-making outfits, kicking out the established gangs by being prepared to resort to the most extreme violence. They represented another side of immigration, an influx importing the hard mentality of the war zone they had left behind and they were using this mentality to take advantage of liberal Western society. To them, Britain's streets were a soft, ripe-for-the-plucking goldmine of illegal cash. Harry had heard them mock their British counterparts. *"Gangs here aren't tough, we're tough. We run things now, no one can fuck with us."* Harry agreed, British gangsters were finished but Serghei was not British and his Somali friends could be out to increase their influence in Tyneside. Harry knew that as well as the trade in drugs, Somali gangs had carved themselves a niche as hit men, carrying out executions for cash. If Harry was removed Serghei and his Somali pals could rule NE England. Harry thought about his latest information. The arms deal in Scotland was being put together by Somalis who were moving the weapons or explosives to Tyneside on Benji's Boat. Benjamin Black was sailing Harry's boat the Delta Queen to Scotland and Harry had just delivered two Somalis courtesy of Serghei to Benjamin. Their mission was to scout out North Berwick and sniff out anyone who looked capable of putting an arms deal together. Serghei had double crossed him. The Somalis already had the deal sorted and they planned to bring the weapons, they intended to assassinate him with, on his own boat piloted by Benjamin Black, Benji's boat. 'Cheeky bastards', he thought. Harry would have to do something. He would have to act quickly. *"Is that little shit Joey Carr part of Serghei's outfit?",* he asked.

"I believe so" replied the interrogator.

"*Then kill him*" ordered Harry.

The interrogator smiled and thought '*Hopefully that negro loving Romanian bastard will be next*'. The interrogator didn't like blacks or Romanians.

Benjamin Black had now reached the open sea. He opened the throttle and set a course for Scotland. He looked at his two new crew members. They were as black as the ace of spades. He felt quite envious if he had been born black then maybe his birthmark wouldn't be as visible? Maybe his dick would be bigger too? Alas he was Black Eyed Benji with the permanent eye patch and he was back on the high seas with his two Somali crewmen whom he had been told had gained some sailing experience in Somalia. Did that make them Somali pirates? Benjamin knew both men were armed and he wondered if they had the balls to use their firepower. He thought they probably did but hoped they would find no cause to. The sailing conditions were good and he settled the boat at 22 knots. In four to five hours they would be in North Berwick. If he could avoid speaking to his Somali crew mates then he would.

Mike Shelly was livid. Shelly had been transferred to the security services three years previously. He had been involved in various high profile operations and had started to make a name for himself. He liked Alex McKenzie and wanted to impress him. McKenzie had requested him for this operation and Shelly felt he had let his boss down. McKenzie wasn't renowned for giving agents second chances and Shelly was determined to atone for his earlier fuck up. He had a thousand excuses but McKenzie didn't like excuses, he preferred results. Joey Carr had been lost because Shelly had been complacent. Traffic jams, equipment failures, personnel issues or any other stupid reason didn't wash. Shelly's car had sustained a puncture and the other car had gone to refuel. Joey Carr had appeared in court quicker than anticipated and when they got there he was gone. Shelly was now back at court under the guise of an operative from Her Majesty's Inspectorate of Prisons for England and Wales (HMI Prisons) the independent inspectorate which reports on conditions for and treatment of those in prison, young offender institutions and immigration detention facilities. Along with a staff member he was checking over the cells, detention records and video footage. He asked for a demonstration on the accuracy of the records and seemingly at random picked the name of a prisoner who had been processed the previous day. *"This gentleman here Joseph Mallard Carr, tell me everything you know about his stay and all the records you have on his detention"* asked Shelley. The staff member had been told to co-operate with the HMI and be as helpful as possible so every scrap of information the court had was passed to Shelly who trawled through it making notes where appropriate. Carr had been released around 3pm. There was nothing of great value on the court's official records. He checked the CCTV footage of the public areas and saw that after his release Joey had been met two males in the foyer. One of the males was using a mobile phone. The video operator had shown some interest in them because he had zoomed in on them with the camera for a short while. Joey then left the court with the two males and the cameras outside showed he entered a blue Vauxhall Astra. Shelly made arrangements for all the data and footage to be downloaded and thanked the turnkey for his help.

Seamus was in custody at Lanark Police Office. He paced about the small cell and hoped that Shemain and Theresa or someone would get him out soon. He had been arrested earlier that morning within the Lanark War Memorial Hall. He was accused of stealing scrap metal from the building which was built in 1926 in memory of the

232 local men who lost their lives in the First World War. The building was currently under a 5 million pound refurbishment but it had been lying empty for years. *"That is not the case officer. Tis a misunderstanding",* he had told the arresting officers. *"I was looking for my cat and I thought it might be hiding in the building so I was just pulling out a few bits and pieces to see if I could find its hiding place."* Seamus was earmarked as a custody case and charged with theft by housebreaking. This was a serious enough crime but it was aggravated owing to the fact he was vandalising a war memorial in his pursuit of scrap metal theft. Both these crimes were highly topical and Seamus had been told to expect no mercy from the Lanark Sheriff who would hear his case. Seamus pressed the buzzer located within his cell and when the turnkey eventually opened the hatch in his cell door, Seamus asked to see the CID.

The turnkey laughed before replying *"Don't worry son. I think they will be coming to see you shortly."*

     Giles Wainwright was trying to make sense of the latest developments. He had nothing tangible in North Berwick to work with. All his enquiries and observations had drawn a blank.

Something did appear to be going on in Newcastle but what? He had discovered an association between two foreign gangsters but it did not merit an operation of this size. The files regarding the boat and crew owned by Harry 'the Turk' landed on his desk. He read through it. The boat was called the Delta Queen. It was a thirty six and a half foot motor cruiser powered by two Volvo Penta Diesel D4 300hp Duoprop Sterndrive engines. With its total 600hp, it could reach a speed of 35 knots. He checked the map and worked out it was about 100 nautical miles from Newcastle to North Berwick. Early indications were that was where it would head. The C35 Sealine Cruiser could hold 750 litres of fuel so it should get there with out refueling if it watched its speed. It was a four berth boat so its three passengers should be fairly comfortable. It was still a fairly tenuous link between the two locations and his sketchy intelligence. He read on. The two passengers had still to be identified but the pilot of the boat was Benjamin Black. He was ex Navy and ex police. There was nothing spectacular in his files but he had been suspected of drug taking before he was asked to leave the police and he had been on the payroll of Harry 'the Turk' ever since. If proof were needed of his drug involvement then his current employment certainly suggested it. Giles was reminded of the intelligence that the police may have been compromised and might not be trustworthy. Did Benjamin Black still have police contacts? This little niggling question reinforced his policy decision to keep the police out of the intelligence sharing process. He read on. Benjamin's distinguishing birth mark had earned him, amongst others, the nick name Black-Eyed Benji. A light went on somewhere in the recess of Giles's mind. Had he found Benji's Boat? He backtracked to the source of this information about the boat. It was in the report from Joey Carr. His last update was that Joey Carr had disappeared. He took a swig from his coffee cup. It was cold. *"Someone get me another coffee"* he shouted *"and get me the analyst's report on that policeman's phone. What's his name, Jamie Douglas?"*

Jamie Douglas had called Alicia earlier. He had arranged to meet her at a coffee shop in town. He walked in and looked around. It was hard to see who was in the shop as it was full of hidden alcoves. A foreign sounding assistant asked if she could help him and when he told her he was meeting someone the assistant led him to the rear of the café where he found Alicia waiting for him.

"*Hi gorgeous*", she announced and welcomed him with an amazing, alluring smile and a cheeky wink. He sat beside her and immediately her hands were in his and she was staring longingly into his eyes. A few tender remarks were exchanged and Alicia released her grip before sliding back along the seat to put just a little distance between them. Jamie went to slide along beside her but she stopped him and motioned to the waitress. "*I'll have a black coffee, what would you like*" she asked Jamie.

He ordered a Coke and a roll and sausage. He wasn't a coffee drinker and he had missed breakfast. "*How many bad boys did you arrest last night, Mr Policeman*?", Alicia said in an alluring but teasing voice. Jamie blushed. "*I know who you should be arresting*", she said and the conversation was directed towards the criminal empire run by Harry 'the Turk'. Alicia would ask a question to find out what if anything Jamie knew about different parts of Harry's operation. Jamie had been checking the intelligence system and he was able to talk fairly knowledgeably about some of Harry's premises or areas of operation. Jamie was able to name a few of Harry's henchmen but seemed blissfully unaware of Harry who liked to stay well below the radar as far as the local police were concerned. She had been briefed by Harry to extract as much information about the police knowledge of his activities and there after to provide misinformation about the operations under his control whilst spreading damaging information about his rivals. She was to give Jamie the impression that local Newcastle gangs were running the show so that the police remained unaware or confused about the foreign influence on their patch. Her briefing was to find out more about the North Berwick angle but she was satisfied Jamie knew little more. She had formed the opinion the previous evening that he was full of his own importance but had a limited knowledge of the Newcastle crime scene. At least today he seemed a bit more knowledgeable and she listened to his analysis of police intelligence. She suggested a few areas where she felt his viewpoints should be corrected and put forward the names Harry wanted the police to think about.

Jamie couldn't help himself he just blabbed to impress. Every so often she would stroke his hand and he would try and move closer. She would politely and teasingly hold him back and say *"Not here*." She talked to him about his work and she knew things about subjects or criminals he was keen to learn about. She was beautiful and he thought she was perfect. They talked for nearly an hour and she left him promising to call later. Tonight she would see him again. He paid the bill and floated back to his car before setting off for the police station where he spent 3 hours on the criminal intelligence system filling it with all the misinformation Harry 'the Turk' had planted in his head. He recorded the source of all these reports as being Sally Demir.

Joseph Fallon and Michael O'Leary had risen fairly early but had not really accomplished anything. Michael had left the flat fairly early touring the shops and checking out the Post Office. He had walked around the town looking for any signs that would indicate there were any serious players in town. He had found none but it was early days. Back at the flat he discussed their progress with Fallon. No one in the Auld Hoose pub had looked remotely suspicious. Their briefing was to look for professionals, killers, mercenaries or gangsters who would have the knowledge and ability to put together a business deal concerning arms and explosives. Fallon and O'Leary would recognise these types of people right away. They lived permanently in the underworld and they could recognise fellow members or players much in the same way as a wolf could sense another member of the pack. It took one to know one and if there were any players in the town of North Berwick they would soon sense them. So far they had found nothing but they were enjoying the rest and relaxation in a thoroughly hospitable and scenic seaside town.

Malky had also been up bright and early. After spending most of the morning on his laptop performing some web editing and design work which was now his chosen occupation he had set off for another scenic dog walk with his little pal and trusty West Highland terrier, Max. They had wandered along the East Bay past the Glen Golf Club and the Tantallon Caravan and Camping Park which was also overlooking the Firth of Forth. The caravan park occupied a truly idyllic location and had unrivalled views of the Bass Rock. He had stayed in the caravan park on many occasions when he had a touring caravan and he had considered buying a static caravan there before he decided to purchase his flat. He reminisced over how he had on many occasions taken the short walk, via a footpath directly from the park, to the beach and then visited the charming harbour town with its varied shops, bars and restaurants which were less than a fifteen minute stroll away. The leisure pool was close by and the Glen Golf Course where 'pay & play' could be arranged was right next to the caravan site which also had its own 9-hole putting green and a wonderful timber built mini-adventure playground. Malky had fond memories of Tantallon and so did his family. Next stop was Tantallon Castle which is a mid-14th-century fortress. It was located just beyond the caravan park. It sits atop a promontory opposite the Bass Rock, and looks out onto the Firth of Forth. It was the last medieval curtain wall castle to be constructed in Scotland. Tantallon Castle consisted of a single wall blocking off the headland, with the other three sides naturally protected by sea cliffs. There was a considerable history to Tantallon Castle and it had been besieged on several occasions through out the centuries. The last siege had taken place in 1650, during the Third English Civil War, when Oliver Cromwell's Parliamentarian forces invaded Scotland, taking control of the south of the country following their victory at Dunbar in September. In February 1651, Cromwell found his lines of communication under attack from a small group of Royalists based at Tantallon. This group, led by Alexander Seton, comprised just 91 men. Despite this, Cromwell's retaliation was to send 2,000 to 3,000 troops under General Monck, together with much of the artillery he had in Scotland, and lay siege to Tantallon. Seton was ennobled by Charles II, as Viscount of Kingston, on the 14th February, during the siege. After twelve days of bombardment with cannon a breach was made in the Douglas Tower. The defenders were compelled to surrender, but only after quarter had been granted to them in recognition of their bravery. After the siege Tantallon was left in ruins: it was never repaired or inhabited afterwards. The siege of Tantallon was also interesting in that the Commonwealth land forces were supported by the Commonwealth Navy. On arrival at the castle Malky was slightly out of breath and in no fit state to lay siege to anything. The clandestine approach which he had undertaken to avoid the entrance fee had taken its toll but had no doubt also burned a few calories in the process. He had eaten no crisps or chocolate since his vow at the top of the Law and he had started eating fruit again. Max on the other hand was revelling in the exercise and he was not overwhelmed by the castle's defences. Lifting his left leg he assaulted the castle wall showering it with urine. It wasn't as effective as Cromwell's cannon but it left its mark. *"Right boy let's head for the County I could murder a pint"* announced Malky. Max declared a truce with Tantallon Castle, wagged his tail and bolted back in the direction of the town. After spending almost two years in North Berwick Max knew exactly where to go when his master mentioned the County.

Mike Shelly had passed on the CCTV footage he had obtained from the South Shields County Court to the technical team. Their work had taken time but they had produced decent photographs of the males Joey had met and obtained the registration number of the Blue Vauxhall Astra car he had entered. In what Mike had considered fantastic work they had also been able to identify the telephone number dialled by the male, on his phone, within the foyer of the court. The picture quality had been good and the camera operator had zoomed in at just the right time as the male stood with the phone in view of the camera and punched in the telephone number. Mike decided Joey's associates must be professionals if they were not using the contacts or speed dial facilities on their phones. The phone that was used would no doubt be a pay as you go, unregistered phone, which would be ditched after a certain amount of calls but now Mike had one number that had been dialled and with that one number he could find out all sorts of things. This was a fantastic stroke of luck and possibly a major breakthrough. Mike's next stop was the analyst who set to work on the phone. The phone number was an unregistered pay as you go phone. A reverse billing check on the number showed it received a phone call at the exact time registered on the court video. The number of the caller was also checked. It was also an unregistered pay as you go phone. Mike now had two phone numbers. He ordered billing and reverse billing on both phone numbers and asked for historic and current cell site analysis on the position of the phone used by the male in the court. This would hopefully give him the current and recent locations of the phone which could possibly lead him to the location of Joey Carr. It would also give a list of all calls made and received by both phones. The analyst packaged all this information together and gave copies to Mike Shelly and the Operation Sigma control room analysts. Mike Shelly studied his reports. The call data was unclear and confusing to him as he had never been trained in how to use it but the location analysis was interesting. The guy who met Joey at court had moved from the court and taken a very non-direct route to Wallsend where the phone had been stationary for most of the night. The other phone had moved between various locations including the Romanian Coffee Shop which was under surveillance and St Peter's Marina both phones had met up this morning for a short period before the first phone returned to Wallsend. Mike Shelly reckoned Joey Carr was holed up in Wallsend. He notified Alex McKenzie before sending out a surveillance and containment team. He then set to work sorting a plan of action and a briefing for those who would be implementing the action.

DS Lawry was informed that there was a prisoner in custody at Lanark Police Office. As the Detective Sergeant in charge of the on duty Q Division, pro-active CID he knew it was his responsibility to interview all persons in custody for crimes of dishonesty or drugs offences. The purpose of these interviews being to clear up any unsolved crimes that the prisoners may have committed and to gain intelligence about who was up to what on the streets. Lanark was at the arse end of Q Division in the Strathclyde Police Area. It was a mainly rural area and probably didn't receive as much attention from the pro-active CID as it merited. The pro-active CID was responsible for targeting criminals and on-going crimes. They dealt with intelligence led, live operations whilst the re-active CID investigated historic crimes. Prisoner interviews were a big part of intelligence led policing so the pro-active CID took on the responsibility for the role. DS Lawry's team were currently busy in the metropolises of Q Division namely Rutherglen and Hamilton. Murders, serious assault or drug dealers were the criminal currency there and DS Lawry had no one to spare for the interview of a scrap metal thief. He had tried to persuade the re-active CID, the community police and the shift plain clothes to carry out the interview on his behalf but they were all busy. DS Lawry had weighed up his options. The Superintendent had been banging on about scrap metal thefts at the morning meetings. Murder, mayhem and the globalisation of drug dealing, fraud and organised crime were swallowing up all the police resources but all the gaffers cared about were petty scrap metal thefts. It was also a Lanark crime and that made it political. His team were accused of ignoring the Lanark area and if he ignored this interview it would be a double bollocking in the morning. For that reason DS Lawry had decided to conduct the interview himself and he was now sitting in front of Seamus, scrap metal thief and proud member of the travelling community in Lanark Police Office's only prisoner interview room. DS Lawry had conducted hundreds of these interviews and gave his usual opening gambit. He was promising nothing. Seamus was marked down for court in the morning and that decision could only be reversed by the duty officer. The purpose of the interview was only to allow Seamus to unburden his sole of un-confessed wrong doings and only if he wanted to. It was highly unlikely Seamus would be released as a result of doing so because the Duty Officer was not in the habit of changing his mind about his prisoners' custody status. Nothing however was impossible added DS Lawry and valuable information always held weight in any negotiations about the custody status of prisoners both with the Duty Officer and the Procurator Fiscal. DS Lawry gave Seamus a cigarette and offered him a light.

"Tank you sir" acknowledged Seamus. *"Tis a terrible business this, sir, me having lost my cat and ending up in that building looking for him, sir."*

DS Lawry smiled. The room was now full of smoke

which was a direct violation of the Strathclyde Police no smoking policy. His smile developed into a laugh. He quite liked travelling folk. He could never trust them but at least they were usually consistent. They were always very polite and always, he suspected, lied through their back teeth. Seamus was not even going to admit the crime he was caught for, never mind any others he had committed and gotten away with. DS Lawry told him to nip the fag as he was going back to his cell.

Seamus stopped him "*I do have some news sir about some guns and stuff, sir, but officer could you spare me another fag and maybe you could see about getting me out once I tell you, sir. It's big, officer. This information could get you promoted sir.*"

The Strathclyde Police no smoking policy was violated again and the information about guns, explosives and North Berwick was passed to DS Lawry. Seamus decided not to include the information about the Special Branch guy making enquiries with the girls but to leave him out. There was nothing to be gained by telling the police something they already knew about. Instead, to keep his story interesting, he flowered up the tale saying he had heard the Real IRA, who were a splinter group from the Provisional IRA and opposed to the ceasefire, were involved. DS Lawry frankly believed nothing Seamus was saying and every attempt he made to get at the original source of the information was fobbed off by Seamus, albeit politely. Seamus seemed most annoyed when he ended up back in his cell but seemed to hold out some hope that DS Lawry may still secure his release. DS Lawry however had regarded the whole exercise as a complete waste of time and told the Duty Officer that nothing of value had been obtained from the interview. He ensured the Duty Officer's notes were updated to prove he had made the effort of interviewing the prisoner which would hopefully appease the gaffers in the morning. He wandered up to the CID room where he updated the pro-active CID briefing note and entered a log in the intelligence system just in case there was any truth in Seamus's story.

The tea time trade in the County was always busy. All the usual faces were sitting in their usual seats or standing at their usual places. Bruce was explaining to Spocky how he could get four nights pudding, for £1.50, out of a Tesco apple pie. Spocky was trying to source Dundee pies from Bod who was getting some for free. The merit of a Dundee pie was discussed over other pies but the fact these Dundee pies were free appeared to be the deciding factor. They liked a good pie though. Jamesie was engaging in economic warfare with Susan the barmaid who had just put his 5p change in the Lifeboat charity tin located on the bar. Donald suggested copper wire had been invented when Jamesie the joiner and Susan were fighting over a penny. The conversation changed to some hapless sole's love life and a suggestion he may have a new woman but this was discounted when it was universally agreed that his new belle had a face like a treble 20 and even the tide wouldn't take her out. Malky walked in with Max as the laughter echoed through the bar. Tea time was noisy in the County but Susan was adept at hearing and serving drink orders. A cool pint of John Smiths appeared in front of him and the till rang in celebration of the transaction. Malky nodded to the charity tin and the change went to support the lifeboats. This was a signal to start on Jamesie again. Over the years Jamesie must have bought a lifeboat with all the money he had put in the tin but that didn't stop the banter. *"Is it true you don't buy an address book?",* Benjy the lobster fisherman jibed *"you just score out the people you don't know in your telephone directory."*

"Aye and your never seasick because you lean over the side of the boat with a ten pence in your mouth", retorted Jamesie.

Emma Ferguson was back on surveillance duty in the County Hotel. Her duties were rotating between the observation post and the field operation. This practice had been adapted to help the field operatives and the observers to identify the locals and any worthy visitors to the pub. Emma now knew the identity of everyone present. Benjy was a lobster fisherman with a boat. Could this be the infamous Benjy's boat that was going to transport the weapons of mass destruction? She didn't think so, in fact she would bet her pension that it wasn't. Malky was an ex-policeman. He had served with Strathclyde Police and so had Emma. She had also been a detective and was serving in the Serious Crime Squad when her application for Special Branch, was accepted. She had never met or worked with Malky but once it was established he was an ex-cop from her old force there was panic that he may recognise her. She was almost pulled off the job but once it was established he didn't know her she was allowed to continue. This was mainly because resources were now so tight. She had made some very discreet enquiries with her old colleagues to find out what she could about Malky but as she had been warned about the possibility of corruption and exposing the operation these had been very indirect as they could not let anyone suspect they were investigating him. Her two closest friends from her Strathclyde days were a Detective Inspector Cathy Mulgrew who was stationed at Govan where Malky had once worked and a Detective Sergeant Peasy Byrne who had once served in the same Division as Malky. She got the impression Malky had been considered a bit of a 'Jack the lad' swanning about jumping from one plain clothes squad to another doing his own thing and taking a large slice of the overtime, expenses and travel budgets in the process. He was the envy of many, a thorn in the side to some and a damn right inconvenience to any administrators or gaffers who wanted a quiet life. In the Job he had the contacts and experience to organise large scale operations but could he be the link between terrorists, corrupt serving police officers and genocide? She doubted it and again she thought that in any bet her pension would be safe. She had also seen George Logan the taxi owner and ex-policeman. He was a genuine guy and there was no chance he could be a threat to anyone or an international security risk. Emma was concerned about this operation. This was a fantastic little pub and if she lived here she would drink in this pub all the time. She was however trained to keep an open mind and this was a fairly easy duty so she kept her eyes and ears open and stuck to her task. She would air her concerns about the accuracy of the intelligence at Alex McKenzie's next briefing but until then she would stay professional and alert. She giggled at the antics of Jamesie, the joiner, who proudly announced "Ah didnae dae wid", and who stepped aside to give her access to the bar. She ordered two vodkas and cola and thought to herself *well as jobs go it's not the worst.* She also wondered how many other Joiners in the world were happy to broadcast the fact they didn't work with wood.

Mike Shelly's teams were in position watching the industrial unit that was believed to have been the last known location of Joey Carr. There was no sign of the blue Vauxhall Astra and the signal from the phone which had been traced to the building had disappeared. Was Shelly too late again? He told his team to rig up some eyes.

Flexible telescopic video cameras were put in place to view the building's interior. It was empty and there were no sign of booby traps. His team went inside. The place was deserted apart from a chair with some ropes attached as if at some point someone had been tied to it. The wall next to the chair was chipped and scuffed. What looked like slithers of wood from a baseball bat were embedded in the wall and a blood spray pattern was visible. More wooden splinters were lying on the ground along with three teeth and some cigarette ends. At the far end of the room was a small metal brazier which had been made from an old oil drum. It had been burning recently but now it only contained hot embers. Mike Shelly surveyed the scene. He wasn't quite sure what he was dealing with here but it would appear someone had been tied to the chair and tortured or even murdered. He was under strict orders not to involve the local police but he couldn't just leave a suspect murder scene. He contacted Alex McKenzie and arranged a covert forensic analysis of the building by Security Service staff. That way if it was a murder the evidence was secured and they could worry about how to get it into the hands of the police later. What Shelley needed to know was if the teeth and blood came from Joey Carr and if so who tortured or murdered him and why? Someone drew his attention to the brazier. There was what appeared to be a lump of molten plastic amongst the embers. *"Do you think that's the phone sir?",* asked a despondent voice.

Benjamin Black was sailing into the West Bay at North Berwick. He had been told the water in the area of the moorings was shallow at low tide, and may even dry out in low water springs. He was also aware that the East Lothian Yacht Club moorings could be exposed to any swell and with the shallow water could be very uncomfortable or dangerous in breaking seas. The sea however was calm and the tide was in far enough for him to moor the boat without any trouble. His two crewmen did indeed know their way about a boat and they assisted him with the mooring procedures. Both his Somali crewmen were anxious to get off the boat and they pondered using a small inflatable boat to reach the shore but the water was shallow and the tide was on its way out so they took off their trousers, shoes and socks and dropped into the chest deep water before wading ashore. Low tide was a few hours away so they should be able to get back without the inflatable raft but Benjamin told them he would have it ready for them just in case. The two Somalis completed their amphibious landing and stepped onto the sands of North Berwick's West Bay. For the time of year the temperature was hot and the sun was shining. Asad & Nadif had been born in Mogadishu which also had a few nice beaches. The big difference between the beaches of North Berwick and Mogadishu was that at this time of year the temperature in Somalia would be around 32 degrees centigrade while North Berwick was struggling to reach 23 degrees. In North Berwick's favour though was the absence of sharks. Anyone watching Asad and Nadif wade ashore would have noticed there heads swivelling and their eyes darting around as they looked for tell tale signs of the Zambezi River or Bull Shark which grabbed many of their Somali victims in thigh deep water. Safely ashore Asad and Nadif began to explore the bustling seaside town of North Berwick. Their brief was simple. Check out the town, analyse the inhabitants, identify if anyone was capable of setting up the kind of deal Serghei and the Turk had described. Any such people would be easy for men with the experience of Asad and Nadif to identify. All they had to do was keep their eyes and ears open and if any such deals were taking place they knew the tell tale signs to look out for. The two big, black Somali gentleman wandered up from the beach into Forth Street. No one gave them a second glance. Chinese, Vietnamese, Eastern European, Asian, American, French, Swedish and even English visitors were embraced by the North Berwick residents and Asad and Nadif blended into the surroundings. Not a single resident saw killers, gangsters, black thugs or potential trouble. All they saw were two more of the multicultural swarm of visitors attracted by the location and beauty of the town. Certain members of the Security Service however were warned of their arrival and almost immediately Asad and Nadif were under surveillance.

Surveillance teams alighted from various vehicles and took up positions using three person or 'ABC' Surveillance techniques. This kept two sides of the subjects covered. 'A' followed the subjects. 'B' followed 'A' and concentrated on keeping "A" in sight rather than the subjects. The normal position for "B" was behind "A." "C" operated across the street from the subjects and slightly to their rear. This enabled "C" to observe the subject without turning his head. The tactics were flexible and 'A', 'B' and 'C' had various options for interchanging to observe the subjects and report on handovers, meetings, pick ups or any other activities they may engage in. Both subjects initially headed west on the High Street before performing a U turn and heading east. The surveillance team were well aware of tactics used by subjects who were tail-conscious and who would suddenly reverse their course to check for followers. They utilised their training and blended, seamlessly with the thronging crowds on the High Street. The surveillance log recorded that Asad and Nadif entered 'Great Escape' a shop which supplied a full range of leisure clothing and footwear. Asad and Nadif were observed looking at surfboards and wetsuits before purchasing two pairs of 'Animal' flip flops. The price they paid, The denominations of the notes they paid with and the fact they were served by a male, referred to as Gordon by other staff members, was noted by the surveillance team who were very good at their job. Nothing suggested the meeting with Gordon held any significance to the wider operation and the most obvious reason for the visit was deduced to be that Asad and Nadif probably thought flip flops would be ideal footwear if they were wading back and forward from a boat on a regular basis. 'Animal' would be the flip flop entry level for a pair of fashion conscious gangsters with a wad of cash. Asad and Nadif wandered eastwards and the surveillance continued.

The small unobtrusive man from Kurdistan was waiting at Frankfurt Airport for a flight to Amsterdam Airport, Schiphol. His personal assistant was kitted out in a midnight blue, custom made, Jay Kos suit which was pattern made from scratch based on Bilal's measurements. It had hand-basted full canvas interlining rolled lapels, surgeon cuffs, pick stitching, hand-molded shoulders and horn buttons. His patterned Salvatore Ferragamo tie, crisp white Forzieri shirt, black Tanino Crisci shoes and Rolex Mariner watch made him look like a top executive. The other two henchmen did not have the class or style of Bilal but they were smartly attired and doing their job. The two bodyguards continued to be vigilant as they set off on the next leg of their journey to Dublin.

Charlie Brandon was still at his desk in the Northumbria Police Intelligence Office. He was now curious about Sally Demir the source of all the intelligence submitted by PC Douglas. Suddenly Jamie Douglas was swamping the intelligence system with information. He hadn't been a regular contributor to the process in the past but in the last two days he had been very active and all his reports were coming mainly from the same source. Charlie searched through all the activity on the system that had been carried out under the ID used by Jamie Douglas. He found PC Douglas had also been viewing a great deal of intelligence in connection with the O'Malleys, the Conways and other notable Tyneside gangsters. Normally Charles Brandon was happy to see young officers making contributions to the intelligence system but everything Jamie Douglas was adding was either vague or contradicted what was already on the system. It appeared to Charlie Brandon that Jamie Douglas was either making all this stuff up or Sally Demir was feeding him a lot of misinformation. Charlie had been unable to find any trace of Sally Demir on the intelligence system but he had obtained some information on her from other sources. The most interesting thing he found was that she was related to one Seytan Yilmaz who was more commonly known as Harry 'the Turk'. Any information held on Mr Yilmaz was restricted to a higher security level than Charlie Brandon could access but there were numerous interest markers which suggested someone was maybe targeting him or looking at his activities. Charlie Brandon noted the necessary reference numbers to enable him to submit an intelligence entry regarding Sally

Demir and her connection to Harry 'the Turk'. In this entry he recorded the telephone number of the phone she had used to contact PC Jamie Douglas.

Giles Wainwright had now been updated regarding Mike Shelly's misfortune in his efforts to trace Joey Carr. The worst case scenario now was that Shelly's initial failure to trace Joey Carr, at the court, may have indirectly resulted in his murder. His DNA matched the blood sprayed on the walls, the blood and gum tissue found on the teeth, and the skin cells found on the rope that had been tied to the chair within the Wallsend industrial unit. This confirmed that Joey Car had at least been tortured there but the question was why? DNA found on the cigarette ends had been identified as belonging to Akhun Adivar. He had also been confirmed from the video footage taken from the court when he left with Joey Carr. Adivar was a known enforcer of Harry 'the Turk'. Up until now there had been no known connection between Harry and Joey but now it would seem Harry needed information from Joey, Why? Joey and Harry had only one other indirect link that he could think of. Both of them had been in the Romanian coffee shop. Could Harry be after information about the Romanians or could he be interrogating Joey on behalf of the Romanians? There were too many possibilities. Giles needed more information to make sense of the situation. The plastic blob found in the embers of the brazier had indeed been the mobile phone which Akhun Adivar had been seen using on the court CCTV system. These guys weren't taking any chances. Phones could be traced and these guys obviously knew that. Giles saw that the analyst who was compiling the phone data was approaching his desk. She was carrying a bundle of charts and looked rather pleased with herself. She spread the charts on Giles's desk and gave a resumé of her findings. The mobile phone number used by Akhun Adivar was used to call two numbers during its short lifespan. One was now believed to have been used by Harry 'the Turk'. The surveillance logs submitted, by the teams following Harry, conformed that he was in the same locations at the same time as the cell site analysis showed the phone to be in those locations. The other number phoned by Akhun Adivar was an unregistered pay as you go mobile used by someone who had also used their phone to contact the number now used by Harry 'the Turk'. This person who had been in contact with Harry 'the

Turk' had also been in contact with PC Jamie Douglas. Giles Wainright frowned he now had another link between Joey Carr and Harry 'the Turk' albeit a very weak link. The analyst continued her resumé. "*In addition I have found a second number again an unregistered pre-pay phone that has been in touch with both PC Jamie Douglas and Harry 'the Turk'.*" Giles frowned again his weak link just got a bit stronger. PC Jamie Douglas was creeping deeper into this enquiry. Could he be the reason why the bad guys expected to stay one step ahead of the police enquiry? His phone went again. The post taking observations on the café had identified PC Jamie Douglas meeting a female who had now been identified as Alicia Celik a high class call girl working for Harry 'the Turk'. Her speciality was compromise, blackmail and information gathering. The listening devices planted in the alcove where they had been sitting had recorded most of their conversation. The conversation had all been about Newcastle crime figures but it appeared Jamie Douglas was smitten by the girl. It was possible he was trying to recruit her as an informant but, if so, he was breaking every rule in the book. Whatever the reason for the meeting, it would appear she was giving him information but more worryingly he was giving away more than he was receiving and he had let slip one of his sources. He had broken several golden rules but the cardinal sin he had committed was naming Joey Carr as a source of information to the police. That, deduced Giles Wainwright was why Joey Carr had been tortured. They wanted to know what he had told the police whilst giving him the message that snitches would be punished. A quick search of the cell site data showed that the second unknown pre-pay phone was in or around the café at the time Jamie Douglas and Alicia Celik were meeting in the alcove, so it was reasonable to deduce this phone was hers. The phone on Giles's desk rang again. This time it was someone looking for the analyst. The analyst took the phone, listened and rummaged through her papers. *"Bingo"* she announced circling the first pre-pay number to phone Jamie Douglas. Charlie Brandon's intelligence report had just identified Sally Demir as the person who had called Jamie Douglas, Harry 'the Turk' and Akhun Adivar. This communication circle now included five people and five telephone numbers. Two of these numbers were no longer operating. The number used by Harry 'the Turk' was also no longer transmitting any signal so Giles deduced it had met a similar fate to the molten plastic consumed in the brazier at Wallsend. Alicia and Sally's phones were still operating, as was the one used by Jamie Douglas, so between the analysts and the surveillance teams they should be able to work out any new numbers used by Harry. For that reason Giles decided not to take any immediate action regarding Jamie Douglas, Alicia or Sally. They were more useful to him staying in contact with each other and more importantly Harry 'the Turk'. He told the analyst to get together with Mike Shelly and sort out how to find Akhun Adivar and Joey Carr. An entry was placed on the Police National Computer to record all sightings of the blue Vauxhall Astra used by Akhun Adivar but not to approach it. The Sigma control room would be informed of any sightings without the police knowing why. Giles wondered where and when the body of Joey Carr would turn up and how the Chief Constable of Northumbria would react if he learned the Secret Service was withholding information about a probable murder in his area.

Joseph Fallon and Michael O'Leary had spent the night moving between the Ship Inn and the Dalrymple bars at the west end of the town. They had drunk a lot of Guinness in very pleasant surroundings but accomplished little else. The intelligence surrounding this venture was looking very suspect but it was a relaxing duty. They headed back to their flat where they retired for the evening.

Asad and Nadif had been exploring the east end of the town where they had been in the Golfers Rest, the Blenheim Hotel and the Quarterdeck pub. They had wandered up to the Railway Station and explored the eastern edge of the town where many of the more expensive houses were situated. They had also popped into the Fly Half bar which was part of the Nether Abbey hotel located at the far eastern end of town. Nothing they saw gave any obvious indications of crime, criminals or weapons deals. All they experienced was a welcome from the residents of a picturesque seaside town, hospitality and good beer. They were now back in the cabin of the Delta Queen and enjoying a beer and a whisky with Benjamin Black. Two pair of flip flops were scattered on the floor.

During their tour of the east end of town they had popped into Lockett Bros, the wine merchant and whisky specialist. The proprietors boasted they loved sourcing, selling and drinking whisky and that they drank it pretty damn well. On the advice of Chris, one of the proprietors, they had acquired a bottle of Glenkinchie. This came from the local distillery which was situated in the rolling, peaceful farmland of East Lothian. It was only 20 minutes from the capital city of Edinburgh and the whisky was known as 'The Edinburgh Malt'. This typical lowland malt, displayed light, floral & fragrant aromas and flavours. This was supplemented with two bottles of Chris's current favourite. A Springbank 10 year old, single malt, matured in bourbon and sherry casks and perfectly balanced from first sip to the full, rich finish. It smelt of orchard pears with a hint of peat, vanilla and malt. It tasted of malt, oak, spice, nutmeg, cinnamon and vanilla essence leaving a sweet finish with a lingering salty tingle. It was exquisite.

Asad and Nadif were enjoying the Springbank whisky. They had nothing to report. They reiterated that North Berwick appeared to be a picturesque seaside town and there wasn't a gangster in sight. They did however have an uneasy feeling that they were being watched but paranoia was the constant companion of the gangsters so they lived their lives on edge. Benjamin Black was now on speaking terms with his two new companions. Their common bond with the sea and the obvious seamanship shown by the two Somalis during the short voyage had impressed Black. He learned that they had both started life as fishermen but foreign fishing vessels who were illegally fishing Somalia's seas and stealing an estimated $300 million of tuna, shrimp, and lobster which were taken each year had depleted stocks previously available to local fishermen. With no Somali Navy to protect their livelihood they progressed to being pirates along with the other local fishermen in an effort to preserve their fishing stock. Soon after they were introduced to mercenaries or ex-militia men and became involved in the business of the Local Clan Warlords who were more interested in financial gain. This had also presented opportunities in other criminal enterprises and brought the two fishermen to the UK where drug dealing, violence and assassinations were now their core business. Benjamin Black had also recognised Asad as a fellow cocaine user and much to the annoyance of Nadif both Benji and Asad were complementing their alcohol with a line of coke. Nadif reflected that this was possibly the reason they had landed this apparently dead end mission. Asad was becoming a liability because of his tendency to use the product he was supposed to be selling, so Serghei had probably sent him here to this quiet town in order to keep him from messing up any proper jobs. Nadif wondered if Harry 'the Turk' had done the same thing to Benjamin Black or was Nadif becoming as paranoid as his two junkie associates. Nadif poured more of the single malt whisky into his glass. *'Who needs cocaine when you've got this stuff?',* he thought.

Jack Stirling was sitting at his covert monitoring post watching the screens linked to the cameras monitoring the County Hotel. The hotel was now closed to the public and as far as he was aware only the manager Ian Steel and a resident Bradley Bone were still in the bar. The camera covering the front of the hotel could see some of the bar area through the front window. Bradley Bone was now visible looking out of the window and pointing directly at where the camera was hidden. Ian Steel joined him and also looked up in the camera's direction. Bradley Bone was intermittently pointing at the camera. Were they looking at him, looking at them? Jack Stirling was getting paranoid it was not uncommon for equipment to get compromised but early indications were no one within the hotel was the least bit surveillance conscious. Surely they hadn't become aware of the cameras already. A note was put in the surveillance log.

Ian Steel was enjoying a pint of Guinness before going to bed. He suspected Bradley Bone was trying to ensure another round was poured before the faucets, beer lines, and keg couplers were cleaned and then switched off for the night.

Bradley was already in the bad books with Nina. A few customers had been making remarks about her proposed role in the Somali pirate nonsense. Bradley had made a public apology conceding that whilst half the world's navies may have been interested in her, she had no interest in them.

Ian listened to his latest nonsense. *"I'm telling you she was at the window this time last night in her bra"* Bradley insisted pointing again in the direction of the surveillance camera and trying to convince Ian there was a gorgeous women undressing for him in one of the opposite windows. *"Give it ten minutes and I bet she comes back."*

Ian ignored him and set to work cleaning the equipment. He wasn't born yesterday and if he waited 10 more minutes that would mean two more beers. Big Bradley would try anything for a free beer. Ian was proud of his reputation for selling good beer. Bacteria, yeast, mould, and beer stone would never get the chance to build up and degrade the quality of draft beer on his premises. He knew routine cleaning was essential to maintain quality and a fresh taste so he made sure it was done. Good tasting beer was a key part of his business plan but supplying free beer to Bradley wasn't. He made a mental note to put some more effort into enticing Stevie Duncan to join the darts team. *'At least he buys some drink,'* reflected Ian.

6 FRIDAY

Alex McKenzie was reflecting over the previous days work. Something was possibly happening that linked Tyneside and North Berwick but it was not exactly obvious. Intelligence suggested that there would be some kind of arms deal taking place in North Berwick but exactly where and when, was not immediately apparent. The movement of a boat from Tyneside to North Berwick could be significant but so far the two men who had disembarked and who appeared to be of African decent, had done nothing to indicate any criminality. A particular cause for concern was the disappearance of Joey Carr and the discovery of a possible murder scene. The association between Harry 'the Turk' and Serghei, the Romanian gangster, added further intrigue to the situation.

Add to that the presence of a suspect policeman who was either cultivating informants in a particularly stupid way or was just plain corrupt and this complicated the circumstances slightly but, so far, no evidence had been obtained that really justified the involvement of the Security Services. The feedback he was receiving from his agents on the ground, in North Berwick, also suggested the Security Services had no business being in this picturesque seaside town. This whole operation had been conceived to investigate and prevent loss of life on a large scale but Alex McKenzie was unsure how North Berwick had any part to play in the forecasted genocide.

Serghei, the Romanian café owner also had reservations about the North Berwick intelligence but he had gone along with it as a favour to Harry 'the Turk'. It never done any harm to have your associates feel they may owe you, thought Serghei. Harry had probably been right to check out the information he had received about weapons and explosives destined for Tyneside because knowledge is power and anything you can find out about your rivals is useful. Serghei and Harry were business associates. Harry sourced a great deal of the illegal commodities sold in the Tyneside area whilst Serghei had always provided the muscle and distribution networks to ensure the relevant markets were serviced. Both parties benefitted enormously but they were independent autonomous operations who complemented but did not entirely trust each other. Serghei believed that Harry used Serghei's organisation to distance himself from the street level customers that bought his merchandise and the forces of law and order that disliked his products. Serghei believed he was the firewall that kept the heat away from Harry and allowed him to operate without unwanted attention. They had worked well together, so far, but Serghei was aware there were other suppliers and distributers in the market place. Harry could change distributers if he felt it was advantageous and Serghei could seek different suppliers if Harry failed to deliver. He was also aware that new firms were trying to gain their share of the market and either he, or Harry, or even both of them could easily disappear if they didn't stay ahead of their rivals. So far, being Harry's associate had worked well for Serghei and for that reason he was happy to work with Harry and gain knowledge which could be vital to stay one step ahead of any rivals. If anyone was gaining weapons to use in Tyneside, he needed to know. Serghei had to look after his own interests. He needed to stay one step ahead of his rivals and for that reason he had recently formed an alliance with the Somalis. The Somalis were an ambitious firm and they were trying to muscle in everywhere. Al Qaida funded them, piracy gave them more money and they sourced weapons from Yemen. This made them powerful enemies or allies and Serghei thought it was better having them as allies. The Romanians were thieves, fraudsters and extortionists. They had a reputation for extreme violence but only when taking on weaker opposition. Serghei had survived in Tyneside because there was no serious opposition but crime was now a global industry and he had to adapt, so he was now in bed with the Somalis and that brought him additional muscle and security. Harry 'the Turk' was however a wheeler and a dealer. If Harry needed muscle, he hired it. Harry had asked Serghei to accompany him to Dublin on another intelligence gathering mission. Some serious weaponry including some secret shit was rumoured to be changing hands there and Harry had made it his business to find out who was involved, what was being sold and why it was being bought. North Berwick was a potential hot spot that had to be checked out but Dublin, Harry reckoned, was where the real action would be. Serghei was now at Newcastle International Airport waiting on Harry and a flight to Dublin.

Rab two as he had been previously dubbed by Rocker Rab or Rab one was enjoying himself in Dublin. He was slightly under the weather this morning as far too many dark rum and Cokes, the night before, had left him just a little hazy. Today was the day and he was clearing his head with several black coffees before continuing with his plan to purchase a run down almost derelict property in the middle of nowhere. Rab had dreams of being the lord and master of his own land. The fact that the only land he could afford was uninhabited and in the middle of nowhere was not, in his mind, a bad thing. Rab didn't need much in the way of comfort. He was a rugged, minimalistic sort of guy. A roof over his head in a desolate place, a bottle of dark rum and access to water and a fishing rod was his idea of heaven. Rab's job took him all over the world and introduced him to all sorts of people but he also liked his own company and wanted a little bit of respite from the materialistic society he was forced to associate with to earn a living. His objective was to secure this little rundown farmhouse with its 15 acres of land and fishing rights on a loch, the name of which he couldn't pronounce, in the middle of nowhere, in Southern Ireland. The property was on the market for 60,000 euro. Rab reckoned that as it had no electricity or gas and poor access he could maybe get it for as cheap as 40,000 euro. He would need to buy a four wheel drive and spend a few quid making it habitable but that was part of the attraction. He was also prepared for a bidding war. In the remote chance that anyone else was interested he was prepared to go as high as 80,000 euro to frighten off any other interested parties. He got his gear together and headed downstairs for the auction which was taking place at the Shelbourne Hotel where he was staying.

The small unobtrusive man from Kurdistan had just finished the last leg of his air journey and was standing outside Dublin Airport. His assistant Jehat Bilal was standing beside him looking suave and sophisticated in his new charcoal gray Brioni suit. One of the minders had been dispatched to uplift the Volvo XC90 luxury automatic four wheel drive vehicle which would suit their needs in

Southern Ireland. The vehicle arrived and the small unobtrusive man entered the rear of the vehicle along with his bodyguard. Bilal got in the front beside the driver. *"The Shelbourne Hotel"* instructed Bilal.

The former IRA Quartermaster General was already in the Shelbourne Hotel. Lot number 42 was the item of interest to him. The catalogue described it as derelict, desolate and in need of rebuilding. He had already arranged a surveyor and viewed the place. There was no sign of anything obvious but this property, he believed, was the key to finding the missing weaponry. The building had to be acquired and shielded from the spying eyes of the British Government who were no doubt deploying every surveillance trick in the book and probably a few that weren't to monitor the activities there. He and his active service units had visited the property several times and every time, he suspected he was being watched but he couldn't prove how or by whom. Visiting the property was one thing but digging up the place without attracting attention was another. If he moved in without authority and began digging up the land, whilst it was under surveillance, he would be investigated and the weaponry would be lost. If he owned the place then that gave him an advantage. Once the prize was located he could deploy anti-surveillance tactics to retrieve and remove the stash. First he needed to acquire the place. He could never bid for it himself though which was why he had brought in outside help.

Giles Wainright was worried. Operation Sigma had provided a lot of interesting intelligence about associations and movements of two Newcastle mobsters but very little else. Intelligence suggested the mass loss of life was to happen next week but they had uncovered nothing about the targets or the plans of the perpetrators and now it was Friday. What did next week mean? How long did they have to sort this thing? He reviewed the latest developments. Harry 'the Turk' and Serghei were now on a flight to Dublin. What did Dublin have to do with the plot? Budget considerations crossed his mind, this operation's costs were mounting. The bean counters at HQ would be on his case soon. He would need to update his section head about his progress. Giles was distracted as another intelligence report was handed to him. *"This appeared on the Scottish Intelligence*

Database sir, our Scottish Counter Terrorist Team passed it on to us. It adds another angle to our investigation" stated the messenger.

Giles looked at the report from Strathclyde Police. The Real IRA was now reported to be involved in the North Berwick weapons deal. The source of the information was an Irish Gypsy and it was graded unreliable by the submitting officer who believed it to be false. Giles pondered for a moment, *'Irish Gypsy provides info and Serghei, a Romany Gypsy, goes to Dublin'*. Giles knew there were links between the two peoples. Through the years Irish travellers have had diverse dealings with Romany Gypsies and both peoples attend important fairs together, such as Appleby Fair in Cumbria in June. This was another tenuous link between North Berwick, Tyneside and weaponry and now the Real IRA and Dublin were involved. The jurisdiction question arose once more. Was this operation now back in Secret Service's territory again? He would definitely need to update his section head.

The sun was shining in North Berwick. Asad and Nadif were out and about. The previous day's exploration had not given them much hope of finding any gangsters in North Berwick so they decided to explore the surrounding area. They walked up from the beach onto Church Street where a number of people were waiting for a bus to Edinburgh. A quick enquiry with the commuters obtained a local taxi number. Asad dialled the number on his mobile phone.

"Hello Jim's Taxi's" answered a friendly voice at the other end.

George Logan was promptly summoned and took a taxi to uplift two gentlemen who wished to explore the area. The Security Services knew the taxi was coming at the same time Asad and Nadif did.

The call from the Home Office was put through to Rupert Basingstoke at the Foreign Office. His opposite number at the Home Office wished to update him regarding the actions taken on the intelligence he had passed to their office on Monday. Rupert was intrigued and listened to how Operation Sigma had been instigated and the developments that had since unfolded. The name of Seytan Yilmaz, also known as Harry 'the Turk', was familiar to Rupert but he never acknowledged this fact to his Home Office counterpart. Seytan Yilmaz was a low level facilitator known on the international scene to be able to source most illegal and occasionally even secret goods. The fact he was in Dublin again interested Rupert but nothing in his voice revealed that fact. "*Interesting report*" remarked Rupert in an offhand manner, "*You chaps appear to be on top of things but the Dublin factor and the suspicion of Real IRA involvement, no matter how tenuous, complicates things. I suggest we take on the Dublin side of things and leave you fellows to follow up things on the mainland. We can't have the Security Services tramping about on foreign soil. It might cause an international incident, eh?*" He chortled. "*Set up the protocols, forward the intelligence and I'll have my chaps take over at the airport. We'll cover the overseas costs but the tab for the mainland side will still be yours.*" Conversation over, Rupert hung up. Picking up the bill for the offshore side of things had deterred his counterpart from insisting on maintaining control of the operation. Controlling the budget deficit was becoming very political and every department had to consider their costs. Every department that was except Rupert's Top Secret Service as no one could afford to cut back on National Security. Operation Chameleon would foot the bill for this one. The UK already had millions of pounds invested in Operation

Chameleon but stood to make billions if the operation was a success. Rupert Basingstoke was already monitoring the activities of Harry 'the Turk' but there was no need for his counterpart at the Home Office to know that.

Whilst Operation Sigma had not yet revealed anything of significance as to the aims of its targets, the mechanisms by which it gained its information were performing exceptionally well. George Logan's hire was known to Sigma before even he knew about it. The conversation between the taxi controller and Asad had been monitored by a covert monitoring post. The surveillance teams observed Asad make the call and enter the taxi. Asad's phone number which related to a pay as you go, unregistered mobile phone had been obtained from Harry 'the Turks' phone records and the analysts were already working on it. A tracking device had been placed on George's taxi so its position was always known but any conversations between George and his occupants remained unknown because Alex McKenzie had been unable to gain authorisation to bug the taxis for the same reasons he had been unable to bug the County Hotel. To break into and bug a property owned by law abiding citizens and freely accessible to the public was not acceptable to the Scottish Courts.

The movement of the taxi was monitored and Alex McKenzie was notified of its progress. The vehicle was heading south on the B1347. McKenzie looked at the available options. The largest populated locations nearby were Haddington or Dunbar but there were numerous farms, small villages and towns in the vicinity. Where could they be heading? The two African males from Tyneside, who were connected to Harry 'the Turk', were now in direct contact with George Logan, who was a possible suspect for being the ex-policeman mentioned in the original report which had sparked off the investigation. Was this significant? Where were they going? Why were they going there and what should he do about it? Because North Berwick was not exactly a sprawling metropolis he had been careful not to flood the town with agents and vehicles as he did not want to attract attention and arouse suspicions. The last thing he needed was for suspicious residents to phone the police about strange vehicles or people loitering in the area. This could alert the police to their presence in the town and compromise Operation Sigma. Normally a floating-box surveillance system based on continuous coverage where the surveillance teams surround their target, blend in and become a part of the target's ecosystem would be used.

The teams would create a box of surveillance vehicles around their target and float with it as it travelled along its route, hence the name floating-box. It was very effective in urban and suburban locations and very few suspects broke out of a properly-run floating-box. This was not however a suitable location for this type of strategy so Alex McKenzie opted for static surveillance which was also based on phased coverage, but used fixed observation posts instead of a floating-box. Each observation post was located at a decision point like a major junction, along the target's route. He knew this method of surveillance left many gaps in coverage but it was also very difficult to detect this type of surveillance. He also had a tracker on the vehicle so he decided to keep his teams out of the target's view in the meantime.

The taxi left North Berwick and headed for East Fortune a village located 6 miles south. George was always pleasant and helpful to his fares so he explained that the area was known for its airfield which was constructed, during the First World War, in 1915 to help protect Britain from attack by German Zeppelin airships. Imparting some more local information he also told them how in 1919 the British airship R34 made the first airship crossing of the Atlantic, flying from East Fortune to

Mineola, New York. George was delighted to show his guests the local sights and continued to act as a tour guide explaining how during World War II the airfield was brought back into service as RAF East Fortune, and he told them how for a short period in 1961, East Fortune operated as Edinburgh's airport while facilities at Turnhouse were being reconstructed. Asad and Nadif listened as George continued telling them how in 1975, the National Museum of Flight was opened at the airfield, and has since become a popular tourist attraction. It was also home to a Concorde, G-BOAA from the decommissioned British Airways fleet, which forms the centrepiece of a major exhibition about the Concorde programme. George stopped outside the airfield. Asad and Nadif Continued to act attentive and learned how at the eastern side of the airfield the old runways and link roads of East Fortune airfield were now used as a motorcycle race track run by the Melville Motorcycle Club. There were around 7 race weekends every year with racing on both Saturdays and Sundays, continually attracting over 200 competitors over the several classes available. Riders travelled from the local area, Northumberland and as far as Ireland on occasions for most weekends. Melville Motorcycle Club ran the track on a not-for-profit basis and had reinvested heavily in resurfacing and upgrading facilities. Asad and Nadif looked at one another this was not what they had in mind when they decided to find out about the local area. George further enlightened them as to how at the western side of the airfield, East of Scotland Micro-lights operate from the extension to the main runway that was laid in 1961 when the airfield was used as Edinburgh's airport. He added that an annual air show is held, normally in July but no aircraft are able to land during the air show because the runways are now in an unfit state for aircraft operations. The running commentary was becoming slightly irksome to Asad and Nadif but they put up with it. Much to their relief George started the taxi again and moved off.

The monitoring post which was following the progress of the taxi on the computerised tracking system noted it was travelling south on the B1347 where it had slowed right down and stopped for 2 minutes outside East Fortune Airfield at the entrance to where the Sunday Market is held. The taxi then headed for the village of East Fortune. Alex McKenzie had opted for the static surveillance tactic enhanced by the tracking device to keep note of the taxi's location. He had reduced the risk of any of his cars getting too close and being compromised but he had not anticipated the vehicle stopping in the middle of nowhere and now that it had, he was worried they had uplifted or dropped off something which he had missed. *"Shit"* He announced *"Get closer surveillance on the taxi and get someone to check out the area where the taxi stopped."* The command was given for the surveillance convoy to gain a visual on the target. The controller running the radio communications gave the order to move to a floating box formation and the radio traffic increased as the commands, instructions and updates to get everyone into position were relayed over the airwaves.

Michael O'Leary and Joseph Fallon were also out and about. They were now convinced that the North Berwick intelligence had been false and the only people in the town capable of putting a weapons deal together were themselves. Their intelligence gathering mission was almost over and they decided they would be leaving North Berwick later that evening or first thing on Saturday morning. They decided to look around the surrounding area and, travelling in their silver BMW, they were heading for Haddington travelling on the B1347.

Emma Ferguson was a fully trained mobile

surveillance officer but she was not on the disposition for mobile surveillance that morning. As an undercover operative who had been detailed to infiltrate the County Hotel she was not wearing her body rig radio set which included a standalone, internally mounted ear-piece and microphone which were virtually undetectable. Undercover officers did not wear radio equipment of any kind. The Volkswagen Golf motor vehicle she was using was not part of the surveillance convoy either and therefore was not kitted out with a vehicle radio set which offered hands-free operation. Her only means of communication with the control room was via a hand held encrypted airwave radio which had been left in her car for convenience. As the surveillance teams got into their positions the excited but controlled radio traffic flowed through the airwaves and she couldn't help but get engrossed in it. This was the most excitement that had occurred in the operation so far and she turned to her partner, Bill Woods. She didn't have to say anything. He was driving and the vehicle was already increasing speed to join in the chase. The command vehicle which was tasked with maintaining visual contact on the target was in position. This pivotal role kept other team members informed of the target's direction, speed, intentions, etc. Emma could hear the back up vehicle was close behind getting into a position where it could take over as command vehicle because the command vehicle was the vehicle most likely to be detected by the target. A number of strategies had been devised to allow the backup vehicle to take over the command role and allow the previous command vehicle to exit the surveillance box. Additional back up vehicles were moving into position. Advance vehicles were also moving into position to provide an early warning system of obstacles, hazards, or traffic conditions that would otherwise catch the surveillance team unaware.

Moving through the village of East Fortune Asad quickly decided it was not gangster territory. They continued on to East Linton where George began to tell them how East Linton was situated on the River Tyne and probably got its name from the Linn, a waterfall next to the village. Asad interrupted him as East Linton did not appear to be a hot bed of criminal activity either. *"Are all the places about here as small and isolated as this?"* When George responded that they were he was told to take them back to North Berwick but via a different route. Asad had already decided they would limit their search to North Berwick.

Various outrider vehicles were now patrolling the perimeter of the floating-box. Their assignment was to make certain that the target vehicle did not get outside the containment of the box. They also played a key role when the target made turns at junctions. Emma Ferguson was not officially part of the surveillance team or their convoy but she updated the controller that she was available in the outrider role if required. The controller was unhappy that an undercover officer, who was unequipped for surveillance, was operating in their surveillance plot but he was also aware that he needed someone to check out the area where the taxi had stopped. He told Emma to break off from the surveillance and check out the area of the B1347 where the taxi had stopped. Bill Woods was also a trained surveillance driver. He had been trained to the highest and safest standards in pursuit driving by elite driving instructors before he was allowed anywhere near surveillance driver training. The elite driving instructors refused to teach surveillance driving because the techniques involved often ignored the Highway Code and did not comply with their ethos of being visible and signalling their intentions to other road users, in particular their targets, to enhance safety. Surveillance drivers often wished to remain invisible and ignored the Highway Code in their efforts to keep up with the target and their convoy. Bill accelerated his 5 door, 6 Speed manual, 2 litre TSI petrol engine shadow blue Volkswagen Golf GTI along the B1347. He kept a 3 Second gap between him and the Caspian Blue Volvo S60 D5 which was accelerating ahead of him. The Driver of the Volvo was an outrider on the perimeter of the surveillance teams floating box. He was ignoring the Highway Code guidance on being able to stop within the clear distance you can see ahead of you. His S60 was travelling at 80mph and the stopping distance was somewhere in the region of 100m depending on various factors. At anytime his view of the road dropped below 100m he should have been decelerating to ensure he could stop in the clear visible area ahead but instead he was using a technique known as half distance acceleration where he accelerated over the first half of the visible distance hoping his visible stopping distance would improve and remain unimpeded but being ready to break firmly if it didn't. Up ahead a left hand bend was looming and the S60 driver adjusted speed, applying constant acceleration to get his car safely around the corner. Bill Woods was using the same technique and followed the S60 into the bend. Emma Ferguson was talking to the controller on the hand held radio. As Bill Woods emerged from the corner he saw the S60 had pulled out to avoid a slow moving silver BMW. Bill was a little slow to react and swerved his vehicle just a little two quickly to ensure proper passenger comfort. As the back wheels began to slide Emma was forced towards the door of the vehicle and she lifted her arms to steady herself and grab the dash board. Her radio was raised to a level where it could be viewed as a result. Bill adjusted the steering, pressed firmly on the accelerator and powered the car out of the skid and passed the BMW. He laughed nervously at Emma's white face as she stared at her radio now blaring on the dash board and looking for a response to the last transmission.

Michael O'Leary was suddenly alert. Being overtaken by a speeding Volvo S60 was not in itself a cause for concern but the close proximity of the Volkswagen GTI and the actions of its passenger caused him to focus on the two vehicles ahead. Joseph Fallon's senses also sprang into action and his instincts warned him of impending danger. Both men had seen the radio in the passenger's hand. Each of them was fully trained in anti surveillance techniques and well aware of the tactics employed by Special Branch and other security organisations.

Joseph Fallon looked around him decided they were not the subject of the surveillance. His initial briefing had mentioned that the Special Branch may be investigating the happenings in North Berwick this seemed like proof they were. He set off in pursuit of the two suspected Special Branch vehicles hoping they would lead him to the people who knew about the weaponry.

George Logan was on his way back to North Berwick in his taxi completely unaware of the attentions of the Security Services. He took Asad and Nadif back via Athelstaneford which he explained was, according to popular legend, where the original Scottish Saltire, the white diagonal cross on a sky blue background, was first adopted. On the eve of a battle between an army of the Picts and the invading English Angles from Northumbria, in 832AD, Saint Andrew, who was crucified on a diagonal cross, came to the Pictish King Óengus II in a vision promising victory. The next morning the Picts observed a white cross formed by clouds in the sky. They won the battle and attributed their victory to the blessing of Saint Andrew, adopting his form of the cross as their flag, and naming him as their patron saint. The leader of the retreating

Angles, Athelstan, was slain at a nearby river crossing, hence the name Athelstaneford. George added that the village is home to the National Flag Heritage Centre. Asad was unimpressed.

Emma Ferguson had recovered her composure but could see nothing of any interest at the roundabout where George Logan's taxi had been stationary for two minutes. The roundabout was on a road which seemed to dissect an airstrip. On either side of the roundabout was a runway. One side even had a sign saying 'Danger-Active Runway Aircraft Operating'. The other side had two signs saying 'Sunday Market' There were no buildings, shrubbery or obvious hiding places in the immediate vicinity and she deduced that if the taxi had uplifted or dropped off anything the supplier or recipient must have met them here.

The B1347 is split by the B1343 and Joseph Fallon implemented a right turn just past the Merryhatton Garden centre to rejoin the B1347. Almost immediately he saw the blue Golf GTI and ensured he remained within the speed limit as he negotiated the roundabout at the airstrip and watched as the two Security Service agents scoured the immediate area. Fallon turned to Michael O'Leary and suggested "*Let's go back to*

North Berwick and let the Shades bring the gees back to us." O'Leary smiled, Shades was a term used in west and south west Ireland. It was derived from the Irish Gaelic term 'Se d'og', pronounced *Shay Dowgs*, meaning 'Little Johns'. It was originally used to describe the Royal Ulster Constabulary. British Army soldiers in Ireland were called 'Johns', so the British controlled police force were called 'Little Johns'. 'Shay Dowgs' became shortened to 'Shades'. Gee was Irish slang for the female genitalia but it was also urban slang for a gangster. Fallon reckoned all non political criminals were fanny's anyway so he used the term to describe any gangster, hooligan or thug he encountered. O'Leary agreed waiting on the Branch to follow the gangsters back to North Berwick was easier than trying to find the centre of their surveillance plot.

As they passed through Drem George Logan outlined that during World War II the former West Fenton Aerodrome, later Gullane Aerodrome became RAF Drem and the Drem Lighting System was developed to assist Spitfire landing. Nadif nudged Asad and gave him a look. He could tell Asad was suffering from drug withdrawal and the history lesson from the well intentioned taxi driver wasn't helping. Nadif hoped some alcohol and a meal would square up his friend. *"Can you recommend a good place for a drink and a pub lunch?"* He asked the taxi driver.

"I certainly can" replied George.

Alex McKenzie had a decision to make. He believed the taxi had either performed a pick up or a drop off at the roundabout. Why else would it stop there for two minutes? The surveillance team who had watched the two Africans leave the boat and enter the taxi were certain they were not carrying anything when they had entered the taxi. That suggested a pick up. Should he call in a hit team to intercept the taxi? He decided to wait and see if they were carrying anything when they exited the taxi.

George Logan took his cab past Direlton Castle and explained to Asad and Nadif how it was one of the few proper medieval castles still remaining today which could be considered as a true traditional castle. He outlined how the castle had played its part on several occasions from the late 13th century when Scotland and England were at war and the castle was attacked repeatedly, changing hands many times, before being partially demolished on the orders of Robert the Bruce. He told how the castle last saw military action during the civil war, and afterwards was left to fall into ruin. *"Later owners maintained the gardens, probably viewing the castle as the ultimate garden ornament and the castle gardens feature in the Guinness Book of Records for having the longest herbaceous border in the world."* He added.

Michael O'Leary and Joseph Fallon had returned to North Berwick. They were looking for the tell tales signs of a surveillance operation which would hopefully point them towards their target. Nothing was plainly obvious but they were patient and everything comes to those who wait.

The surveillance team reported the taxi had turned right following the A198 onto Station Road. It turned left onto Marmion Road, into Bank Street and onto St Andrew Street before passing the ruins of the Parish Church in Kirk Ports and stopping outside the rear entrance to the County Hotel. Alex McKenzie was now forcing himself to stay calm. Events had all now turned the full circle and the focus of the whole operation was now turning back to the County Hotel where it had all started. He waited for word on whether anything was being removed from the taxi. He would then have to decide whether to let things run or whether to call a strike.

George Logan alighted from his taxi and walked towards the back door where he had spotted Ian Steel. Under the gaze of surveillance officers and cameras George passed the time of day with Ian and talked of his impending holidays. George introduced his passengers and told Ian they were looking for a bite to eat and a beer. Ian shook hands with his new patrons and motioned them inside. He waved farewell to George who jumped back into his taxi and drove off.

Word came through the two Africans had left the taxi and were entering the County Hotel. The taxi driver, George Logan, had introduced them to the hotel owner, Ian Steel, and it was confirmed they were not carrying anything. McKenzie pondered over how the whole thing had indeed turned full circle and he was back where he started with a hotel owner, a taxi driver and a Newcastle connection but he still had no idea of what they were up to. That piece of the jigsaw still eluded him. The taxi driver had driven them about 15 miles to get them to a hotel about 500m from their pickup point. It was either a fairly obvious taxi fare fraud or the stop at the airfield was significant, but why? They had entered the taxi with no obvious items and left the vehicle with nothing noticeable. What on earth were they up to? McKenzie gave the order to keep the taxi under surveillance and get the undercover team into the hotel.

Michael O'Leary and Joseph Fallon never saw the taxi or its occupants arrive back in North Berwick but they saw Emma Ferguson and Bill Woods enter the County Hotel via the front door in the High Street. *"Let's see who the shades follow out of there and that's our men"* said Fallon in a most satisfactory tone.

Harry and Serghei were now at the Shelbourne Hotel. The crowds were gathering but Harry's contacts had ensured him access. Harry had been directed to the Shelbourne by his associates who had arranged for him to assist with a small acquisition. Serghei was unsure what was happening but if Harry wanted to buy a house in Ireland that was his business. A catalogue of the properties on sale had been handed to Serghei and he leafed through it. There certainly appeared to be a few bargains on offer.

The Irish property bubble had burst in a spectacular fashion but an IMF bailout and swingeing austerity measures had not dented the Irish enthusiasm for a property deal. The crowds spilled on to the pavement at Ireland's latest auction of 'distressed property' as hundreds of would-be buyers flocked to the swish Shelbourne Hotel in search of a bargain. With 84 keenly priced lots, ranging from a three-bed semi priced as low as 22,500 euro to a four-bed mews house in Dublin's most salubrious district going for 600,000 euro, it was always going to be busy but Rab was getting worried and he hoped his derelict, isolated farmhouse wouldn't attract too much attention. He was glad he had made the appropriate arrangements and stayed at the Shelbourne Hotel or he may never have accessed the auction. There were too many people to fit in the Ballroom and initially the quick-thinking auctioneers had dispatched a man with a microphone to the steps of the hotel to relay bids from the pavement back into the ballroom but the police had not been impressed and the auction was briefly suspended to allow the Garda to disperse the crowd outside. Rab approved of this brief hitch which eliminated a lot of would be buyers. Inside, the atmosphere was bristling with excitement as the hammer came down on the first lot, a 500 square foot studio apartment in the centre of Temple Bar, Dublin's equivalent of Soho, a touristy district best known for boozy stag and hen parties. There were at least a dozen bidders. It had a reserve price of 80,000 euro, but it was swiftly sold for 127,000 euro. Rab broke into a cold sweat. He thought it might be the after effects of the dark rum but suspected it was panic induced as the first lot had gone for more than the guide price and things were not looking good. The next lot was a property in Ballsbridge, Dublin's most sought-after residential district, but the four-bed mews house did not attract a single bid at the guide price of 600,000 euro. Rab breathed a sigh of relief as the hammer came down on the former 2.5 million euro property which had just sold for a measly 550,000 euro. He reckoned his farmhouse was still a good bet. His emotions went through a rollercoaster ride as some properties fared better than others. A three-bed penthouse in Bride Street, just minutes the Royal College of Surgeons on St Stephen's Green went for 50% more than the reserve price. Two apartments in Portlaoise, an unprepossessing midlands town about an hour away from Dublin, and best known for its high-security prison which was home to IRA prisoners in the 1970s and 1980s sold for almost double the guide prices whilst some properties never sold at all. After about three hours Lot 42 eventually came up for sale and Rab got ready to take on anyone else who displayed an interest in his dream house. Number 42 appeared on the screen next to the auctioneer who announced Lot 42 was now open for bids. The property was listed in the guide at 60,000 euro. Rab hoped no one would start the bidding at that price. No one did and the asking price was dropped to 55,000 euro. The reserve price was not disclosed but Rab reckoned the bids could fall to at least 30,000 euro before he needed to worry about the property being withdrawn.

"Do I Hear 50,000 euro?", asked the auctioneer.

Rab decided he would start bidding around 40,000 or just slightly less if no one else did.

"45,000 euro" enquired the auctioneer.

It was looking good. Rab began to think he should let the bid fall to 30,000 euro but worried that this may attract unwanted interest because of the low price. He would need to be careful.

"Do I hear 40,000 euro?", boomed the auctioneer.

It was decision time. Rab decided 5000 euro would

be better off in his pocket than in the pocket of the auctioneers he would wait for one more reduction on the bid.

"Will anyone give me 35,000 euro?", pleaded the auctioneer.

Rab was tempted to wait but thought now was the time to make his move.

"35,000 euro" a Chinese voice echoed from the corner of the room.

Rab swirled to see who was suddenly interested in his dream home.

His fears were realised.

Rab was not the only one interested in the prospective buyers of Lot 42. Crispin Oaksey represented the owners of the property. He was not known to the auctioneers or any of the bidders. He was there only to view the proceedings and report to the owners. Crispin was a well travelled man with a good knowledge of many of the players on the international markets, be it property or otherwise. He scanned the room looking for anyone of interest. In the far corner of the room was the Chinese delegation who had just bid. Their presence was expected but Crispin had been unsure if they would bid.

*"Bidding has started at 35,000 euro. Do I hear 40,000 euro? "*asked the auctioneer.

Crispin looked to the other corner of the room where the former IRA Quartermaster General was sitting and wondered if he would be the next to make a move. Would Harry 'the Turk' make the next play on his behalf?

"40,000 euro", boomed Rab. His voice sounded a lot more confident than he was. He took a deep breath.

Crispin was aware that a new player was on the scene, a guy who actually wanted the place. He wondered how much money the fool was willing to spend on it.

"We have forty, that's 40,000 euro do I hear forty five, forty five anyone? Forty is the bid, going once", announced the auctioneer.

Rab started to expel his breath. Crispin scanned the room for any other interested parties. The Russians and Americans were also keeping an eye on proceedings.

"45", the Chinese were back in the game.

"*50*" shouted Rab, hoping his swift reply would announce he meant business. What did the Chinese want with his little fishing sanctuary? He breathed in again.

Crispin wondered what Rab wanted with a desolate plot of Irish bog land.

"*We have fifty, that's 50,000 euro do I hear fifty five, fifty five anyone? Fifty is the bid, going once, going twice*", proclaimed the Auctioneer.

Rab began to breathe out.

"*Fifty five*", the Chinese weren't bowing out gracefully.

"*Sixty*", Rab put himself back in the mix. He took a deep breath.

"*We have sixty, that's 60,000 euro do I hear sixty five, sixty five anyone? Sixty is the bid, going once, going twice*", broadcast the auctioneer.

Rab didn't breath out this time. He held it.

"*Sixty five*", the Chinese, it seemed were serious players.

"*Eighty*", blurted Rab. This was his last throw of the dice. He stared across the room at the Chinese delegation who were bidding against him. Crispin anticipated his paymasters would be amused at higher prices being offered for the property because of this rogue bidder .

"We have eighty, that's 80,000 euro do I hear eighty five, eighty five, anyone? Eighty is the bid, going once, going twice", stated the auctioneer.

Rab continued to stare at the Chinese, daring them to make another play.

"For the third and last time...", continued the auctioneer.

"Eighty five", announced a voice from the other end of the room.

Rab turned in dismay. Another dream house had slipped from his fingers. Crispin smiled. He wondered how long it would take for Harry 'the Turk' to join the bidding.

Rab turned and headed for the bar. He needed dark rum.

"Sold" announced the auctioneer. Crispin watched as Harry 'the Turk' sent his bidder to complete the purchase slip and settle the 10 percent deposit. All the other players were watching too; the Chinese,

the Russians, the Americans and the Irish. Everyone was playing for high stakes and all of them had a plan. Rab had possessed more of a dream than a plan but his dream was now smashed. Everyone else's plans however were still intact. Having secured the help of Harry 'the Turk', the Irish were now the lawful owners of the desolate farmhouse. That was what everyone else wanted even if the Irish were not supposed to know that. No one had told the Irish they were supposed to win and the Irish were feeling pretty good about things. The property transfer would take about five weeks but they now had an excellent reason to start sniffing about the property without harassment and that was where they intended to be first thing next morning. Unbeknown to them so did everyone else. Crispin spotted a rather small unobtrusive man of Kurdish appearance leaving the hotel in the company of a tall sophisticated gentleman in a Tom Ford, two button, solid navy suit. The gentleman was checking his Omega 42mm Planet Ocean watch as he left. Crispin smiled everything was going to plan.

Michael O'Leary and Joseph Fallon were also checking their watches. As far as they were concerned everything was still going to plan. The Shades hadn't reappeared from the County Hotel so the gees must still be in there. Fallon reckoned the whole place would be under surveillance so he had initially thought about using a table on the pavement outside the No 12 Quality Street café bar or the adjacent Dalrymple Arms as a vantage point. Unfortunately there was no way he could gain a view of the front of the County Hotel from there but he could monitor both the junctions at Kirk Ports and the High Street where anyone leaving the hotel and heading east would pass. He had instructed O'Leary to park the car in the corner of the Glebe Street car park where he could cover the other exits from the back of the hotel. It wasn't the ideal scenario and if anyone left the front of the hotel and headed west they could leave undetected so O'Leary was repositioned on foot in the lane at the bottom of Law Road in an effort to cover anyone heading west on Kirk Ports or the High Street. They were both experienced in the art of surveillance and quickly decided the vantage points would have to be changed. Their aim was to identify the gangsters without being rumbled by the Shades who were watching the gees but circumstances dictated they would have to risk exposure as two of them could not cover all the

Etherick Brown

exits without moving closer to the Hotel. Hopefully the shades would be too busy watching their gangster targets to notice they too were the subject of a surveillance operation. Fallon tried to loiter and mingle in the High Street where he could see the front of the hotel and O'Leary plonked himself on the wall of the Old Parish Church graveyard where he could see the rear of the hotel. Both of them felt exposed but hopefully they wouldn't have to hang about too long before the would-be gangsters left the hotel. Fallon went over the possibilities of escape for their targets, who ever they may be. He thought about a story O'Leary had once relayed to him about one of his many female conquests when her father and brothers had wanted to cause him some damage because he had tarnished her honour. He was being chased through the streets of an Irish town when he ran up an alleyway and nipped into the backyard of an undertaker. The fathers and the brothers scurried about outside searching the cul-de-sac and probing doorways certain they had O'Leary cornered somewhere in the blind alley. More of the brothers covered the streets on either side of the dead end. At that point a hearse, with a coffin on display bedecked in a floral tribute to Granddad, emerged from the funeral parlour yard.

204

O'Leary's pursuers had stood to attention and bowed their heads as the casket went past them before renewing their attempts to find and put O'Leary in a coffin himself. They were too late. The shifty bugger, showing a complete lack of respect for the dead, had bunged the undertaker a tidy sum to dump grandpa from his coffin and give O'Leary a ride to safety in his place. His assailants never worked out how they lost O'Leary but his friends had the habit of referring to him as 'Dracula' after hearing of his tasteless but amusing getaway. Fallon was certain his quarry wouldn't be escaping in a hearse but he was worried they may disappear in a vehicle without being noticed.

Asad and Nadif were unaware they were anyone's quarry at this point. As far as they were concerned they were the hunters and not the hunted. Their trail however had gone cold but they suspected it had never been that hot in the first place. They were directed into the bar and shown to a table at the rear of the pub where they were waited on by Stevie, the restaurant manager, and provided with menus. Nadif could see Asad was in need of medication but doing drugs here was not a smart move. He hoped a couple of drinks would square him up. Stevie liked to indulge in a bit of banter with his guests and the two large black African visitors didn't escape his wit.

"Do you serve drinks?", asked Nadif.

"Yes, sir we serve anyone", replied Stevie.

Andy Spence, a regular customer at the next table, groaned but having additional attention encouraged Stevie to indulge in more of his witless humour. He draped the table cloth he was holding around Andy's neck and tapped his bald head which poked through the open end of the table cloth. *"There Andy you look like a burst condom",* he jibed.

Andy remained dignified, *"don't be jealous of my sleek, practical hairstyle just because next door's cat has coughed up better looking ones than yours."*

Nadif saw the small stocky, bespectacled, curly haired waiter, was smiling at him and he couldn't help smiling back. He had initially thought Stevie was being rude but realised he just fancied himself as some sort of wise guy.

Stevie temporarily stopped his stand up routine and returned to his waiter role. *"What can I get you sir?"* He asked Nadif.

This was their first visit to Scotland and Nadif indicated they wished to try a Scottish beer but added that their preference was lager. Stevie suggested two pints of Tennent's lager and explained it was Scotland's best-selling pale lager, accounting for approximately 60% of the Scottish lager market.

Andy Spence choked on his steak pie. It was nothing to do with the steak pie, which was excellent having been made from tender chunks of Scottish beef in delicious gravy and served with fresh vegetables and potatoes. It was Stevie's informative response that amazed him. He must have been watching the recent television adverts which highlighted the lager was first brewed in 1885 by Hugh Tennent, and in 1893 it won the highest award at the Chicago World Fair .

Nadif enquired about the taste and Andy listened to see if Stevie had indeed discovered the secrets of excellent customer service. He waited for the elegant descriptive account from a connoisseur of pale lager describing it as a distinctive, well-balanced lager with sweet, malty flavours combined with a tangy hoppiness which creates a crisp, refreshing character.

Stevie replied *"Aye it's cold and it hits the spot."*

Andy sniggered, the real Stevie was back.

"If the light reflecting off that dome is dazzling you sirs" Stevie asked Nadif and Asad whilst pointing at Andy's bald head, *"we can supply sunglasses."* He disappeared to fetch the two lagers.

Andy got talking to Nadif and Asad about the waiter service.

Emma Ferguson and Bill Woods joined the throng at the bar. The pub was busy and the seated area at the rear was filled with diners. They observed Nadif and Asad were sitting at a far away table. Emma couldn't hear what they were saying but they were laughing with the staff and one of the customers. They looked quite relaxed and comfortable at their table which gave them a view of the whole pub. Emma wondered if they were known here. Sitting at the rear of the pub with their backs to the wall they were in the ideal position for a meeting. They could see everything but the noise from the crowd meant no one could overhear their conversation. She looked at the bald guy at the adjacent table. She recollected he was

Andy Spence. The bald head gave him a distinctive hard man look but nothing known to the authorities suggested he was anybody's 'muscle' or any kind of player in the terrorism arena. The door adjacent to the bar which gave access to the hotel area opened and Bradley Bone appeared. Emma recalled he was the guy with the Newcastle connection. She saw he appeared immediately to notice the bald guy or was it the two Africans. He headed straight for the dining area and sat down at Andy Spence's table next to the two Africans. A Geordie in North Berwick was now sitting next to the closest thing she had seen to 'muscle' in the town and they were adjacent to two African gangsters who were working for a Newcastle kingpin. *'What the hell was going on? I'd love to know what they're saying'* she thought.

Bradley Bone was on a mission. It was a seriously tricky exercise and he needed help to have any chance of securing his objective. Tonight was the night. All the planning and preparation had been done with tonight in mind but there had been a hiccup. Even the best laid plans could come undone and his were now seriously compromised. He could no longer accomplish the task on his own and he needed help which was why he had summoned assistance. As he sat down at the table the two African guys gave him a nod. Bradley got the impression Andy had been speaking to them and nodded back. Assistance was vital to the success of the operation if the relevant threats to his plot were to be eliminated. He pulled his mobile phone from his pocket and loaded an image of what he needed taken out.

Emma Ferguson and Bill Woods watched the interaction. Something was happening and they needed to know more. Bill Woods was dispatched to the gents' toilet to pass their table and see what he could glean from their conversation. He noticed Bradley Bone was showing his phone to Andy Spence. *"That's what I want you to take out"* he overheard Bradley say. Bill strained to see the image on the phone but it was angled in such a way that he couldn't see the screen. *"Fuck's sake that's big"* replied Andy. Bill Woods reached the toilet door which was just beyond the table. He pulled on the door knob instead of pushing it and then fiddled with the handle to try and gain a few more seconds of listening. *"I take it I'll be compensated appropriately?"*, he heard Andy ask. *"I've got the finances sorted but I will need another five for transport"* replied Bradley *"I've just to finalise the time. Can you be ready for half eight?"* Stevie arrived at the table with two Tennents Lagers. Bill Woods decided he couldn't fiddle with the door handle any longer without looking suspicious so he entered the toilet. Flash and Reno, two of the locals were standing at the urinals. To blend in with his cover Bill was forced to take the space adjacent to them. *"Aye that's the seal broken"* Reno remarked *"I'll be pishing for Scotland now. All that beers gonnae come flooding oot."*

"Well don't visit the loo too much because Confucius say man who hang about urinals too long, he feel cocky" retorted Flash. He nudged Bill Woods looking for a response to his wisdom and laughed at his own joke.

Bill Woods felt awkward. He thought he could have managed a pee when he entered the toilet but now that he had to perform with an audience he had lost the urge. These guys were all cracking jokes and if he just left without relieving himself they might think he was only there to 'feel cocky' as Flash had so eloquently put it or even worse they might rumble him as an undercover officer just because he couldn't piss. His awkwardness increased as footsteps and whistling behind him made him aware that someone else needed a piss.

Ian Steel stopped whistling and bellowed, *"Right you wankers, move over and let the big boys in*."

Bill Woods just knew he could stand there pointing his manhood at the urinal all day and not a drop of piss would flow from it whilst these guys were providing an audience.

The sound of breaking wind interrupted his concentration. He left the urinal making room for Ian but still needing a piss and unable to let it flow.

"Oh the Hibbies are gay" sang Ian at the top of his voice as he blasted the urinal with a jet stream of pee whilst musically articulating his thoughts about his beloved Hearts greatest football rivals.

Bill Woods was a 'Toffee Nose'. He was born and bred in Liverpool's affluent Woolton area and where football was concerned his allegiance lay with Everton. He knew of Hibs or Hibernian FC but the term Hibbie did not immediately associate itself with football in his mind. His sport was rugby and St Helens were his team. He became paranoid that the 'Hibbies are gay' reference was something to do with him hanging about the urinals without urinating. He quickly got back out into the bar area.

Emma was wondering what was keeping Bill. Her observations had indicated a significant interest in the phone which had been passed briefly to the two Africans as if some opinion of its content had been requested from Bradley and Andy. It also appeared that money was exchanged between Andy and Bradley but she couldn't see how much. There had been a fair bit of nodding between them before Bradley had apparently indulged in a bout of texting which encapsulated Andy's attention. Emma suddenly felt someone place their hands on her hips.

"Awright Doll?", uttered a voice behind her and she felt someone brush up against her rear. She turned quickly and saw Pablo the good looking drunk with no teeth. He smiled at her and she noticed that in fact he only had one tooth missing. It appeared a crown had come loose and had not yet been replaced. *"I'm trying to get past you"*, he intimated. She realised that she had become so engrossed in the activities at the far table that she had drifted into the middle of the passageway between the bar and the seating area. The space she had left for

people to pass was so narrow that Pablo had little choice but to try and squeeze past her. She smiled back at him and tried to move back in an effort to give him more room but it was still a tight squeeze. As he passed, her hand brushed against his stomach and to her surprise rippled over a pronounced, firm six pack. This guy was fit. *'Could there be more to him than meets the eye?'* she wondered. As her eyes followed Pablo's figure towards the toilet she suddenly noticed there was activity at the table where her targets were sitting. She had been distracted by Pablo but she was now fully alert. Everyone was standing, shaking hands and her targets appeared to be leaving. Pablo's bum was delayed again on its journey to the toilet. It was time to go, which was a pity. Pablo's bum looked as firm as his 6 pack. She would like to have watched it just a little longer.

Bill Woods walked straight into the subjects of his surveillance operation. Asad and Nadif brushed past him into the Gents toilet where they were met by another verse of musical folklore highlighting the sexual orientation of a Leith based football club. Asad had decided he wasn't in the mood for eating. His drug dependency had seriously curtailed his appetite and had got the better of him. He had almost been tempted by the 'From the Chargrill' section of the menu which listed the various quality Scottish meats on offer. Nadif had been on the verge of ordering two fillet steaks with whisky sauce when Asad had said, he had to leave. His urge for drugs was stronger than the need for a good meal. The lager had temporarily squared up Asad but he would have to get back to the boat for another fix. Having just left the toilet Bill Woods was now confused about what to do. He couldn't possibly follow them back in or that would look really suspicious. Andy Spence and Bradley Bone were leaving the bar. Bill stepped back and allowed Pablo to enter the toilet. He saw Emma look at him in exasperation and he wondered who he should follow. Bradley and Andy had used an exit that meant they could go anywhere. The rest of the team were unaware that Andy and Bradley were plotting to take out a large scale target at eight thirty. Bill looked at his watch it was 8pm. In half an hour something big was going to be taken out. He decided Andy and Bradley were now just as important as the two Africans and decided to follow them. Reno and Flash returned to the bar from the hallway door. The Gents toilet had two entrances and because of the congestion at the bar door they had re-entered the bar from the hallway into which Andy and Bradley had just left. Bradley went straight up stairs to his hotel room whilst Andy went outside and straight up to his flat above the hotel. By the time Bill Woods got past Flash and Reno his quarry had disappeared. All he could see was Conrad Campbell, Pablo's brother and Ronnie, Ian Steel's son-in-law, standing at the back door discussing the big news that Stevie Duncan was joining the darts team. As Emma joined him, Asad and Nadif left the gents and made for the front exit. Bill would have to report to someone about Bradley and Andy but he couldn't let the Africans go either. Emma told him to get moving. Bill looked at his watch it was 8.10pm. As he left he saw a tall, slim, blonde women and a grossly overweight brunette standing with two young children. Had it not been for the children he would have said they were up for a night on the town. The blonde looked quite nice in her short skirt and high heels but the brunette in her black dress with gold speckled nylon encased hoover bag legs and white shoes looked positively repulsive. Bill refocused his attention on his surveillance. The two Africans were heading west on the High Street and Bill took his place in the complex web of surveillance tactics that would keep note of their movements. It was 8.14pm and he was worried that his inability to communicate with his control room may result in a large scale target being eliminated at 8.30pm. Once the proper surveillance team was deployed he would have to update the boss.

Joseph Fallon saw the two Africans leave the bar. Seconds later Emma Ferguson and Bill Woods appeared. *"Begorra that's our gees"* muttered Fallon as he watched the surveillance plot form around the Africans and move west on the High Street. A tall guy, in his early thirties, who was at least six feet three with broad shoulders, dark hair and a small paunch possibly obtained through drinking too much beer appeared from the doorway of the County Hotel and took umbrage with the tall slim blonde in the short skirt and high heels. Fallon smiled, he appeared to be upset because she had brought the kids or was it because she had brought the big brunette with hoover bag legs. '*Fuck Ah wouldnae ride her into battle*' he mused. A minibus sized taxi appeared and the tall guy ushered the women and children inside and followed them. Before the door closed Fallon heard a Geordie accent say to the taxi driver *"Wallyford"* and then the taxi was gone. Fallon fell in behind the surveillance plot to see where the gees went.

Andy was putting the finishing touches to his look. It was 8.20pm and he slipped his newly ironed shirt over his deodorant sprayed body and freshly shaved head. Andy had seen the text. She didn't mind bald guys and she was up for some fun. Big Bradley needed someone to take care of his bird's mate on a double date and Andy didn't mind helping out a pal. *'Yes, helping out a pal,'* he thought, that was his excuse for dating a fat bird. Why did Bradley have to show the whole pub the photo? Fuck he didn't even know the two black guys at the next table but he had insisted on showing them the pictures of Andy's blind date. *'What a pair of tits'* thought Andy and she had a nice smile so if she was up for some fun then who cares what the black guys thought. *'Who cares what anyone thinks?'* He decided. *'The female sex weren't exactly knocking his door down to worship his body'*. It was 8.25pm and he didn't want to be late. Big Bradley said that tomorrow he might take his bird to Newcastle if all went well but tonight he needed someone to keep her mate amused. Andy strolled down the stairs and wondered if some serious romance was coming his way. On entering the bar he searched for big Bradley but he was no where to be seen. Billy and Eva another two of the County's locals had just entered and were ordering drinks. Andy asked Kieran, the Irish barman, if he had seen big Bradley. Eva interrupted saying that she had just seen Bradley get into a taxi with two women and a couple of kids. "*Aye and he was in a foul mood*" added Billy who went on to relay a story about Bradley giving this poor women hell because her baby sitter was running late and she had no one to look after the kids till half nine. Bradley had apparently told her to forget her night out and they had all disappeared in the taxi. Andy was livid. His romance had been doomed even before it started because big Bradley was an impatient, selfish, sexist child hater. Andy had been stood up by an obese female he'd never met and he was devastated. "*Vodka and Coke Kieran, make it a double*" he pleaded. It was 8.30pm.

Jack Stirling, in his covert monitoring post, had watched Asad and Nadif leave the County Hotel. They were now being watched by the surveillance teams but another male had captured Jack's interest. He had been hanging around outside the hotel and there was something familiar about him thought Jack who had previously worked on the Irish Terrorism Desk at Special Branch. He dispatched someone to check him out. After that he was left with his CCTV monitors watching the night life which made North Berwick a vibrant little town on a Friday night.

7 - SATURDAY

Rocking Rab Grantham was hoping for a vibrant Saturday night as today was the celebration of his 55th Birthday. He had no work on Sunday and he planned to celebrate the event in style. He looked at his reflection in the mirror and saw an aging rocker who could have taken the world by storm if only he'd been discovered. Jeff Beck, Jimmy Hendrix, Pete Townsend or Angus Young, he could play them all. Rocker Rab was a maestro on what was possibly the most influential instrument of our time, the air guitar. Whilst anyone could pick up an air guitar Rab knew it was spirit that made great air guitarists. There was a certain art involved, in knowing how to make it look awesome and Rab believed he had mastered it. He spun his baseball cap pointing the peak backwards on his head and he unbuttoned his red tartan shirt exposing an AC/DC tour T shirt. Good metal or rock music with the right pace, energy and rhythm were essential to good air guitar playing. He identified an appropriate song with a guitar solo section and some good riffs. He imagined himself creating the sounds and visualised himself being the centre of attention, on stage at the County Hotel, with the crowd hollering for more. He flicked through the tracks on his CD player and selected AC/DC, Dirty Deeds Done Dirt Cheap. He turned the volume as loud as he dared because he knew that when the air guitar was played the music had to be as loud as you, and those around you, could withstand. It was best that way! He went to great pains to get his stance right. His legs were spread wide. He bent his knees a bit and put his right hand about level with his crotch. To hold the guitar in place he bent both arms between 75 and 90 degrees. His crotch hand was in front of his belt buckle with his palm facing the appropriate fret spot whilst his other hand was up in the air with his fingers spread, bent and pointing towards him. He began strumming and fingering the 'frets'. His hand moved lower for the high notes but it never came down too low. Rab knew that no real guitar player would play with the guitar down to their knees, except maybe Fieldy from Korn. Occasionally he caressed the imaginary neck of his guitar, running his hand up and down. It was time to get moving. His whole body got involved. He went for the jerky movements and slides across the 'stage'. He gave special attention to the orgasm-face-pulling solos whilst performing his exaggerated strumming motions. Rab also liked to add some lip-syncing. This step was optional for air guitarists but he knew it was essential to help maestros get into the spirit. He added some loud 'woos' and hollers which he considered mandatory. The shouts from the kitchen and the banging on the walls interrupted his performance. *"Yes dear I'll turn it down"* he shouted. The music was turned off and he headed downstairs but not before he took the rapturous applause of his audience and finished with a bow. Rab was arguably North Berwick's greatest and most influential air guitar player of all time and today he would be performing live at the County Hotel even if the staff knew nothing and had never advertised his forthcoming performance, Rab knew everyone would expect it.

Rab wasn't the only influential person wondering what sort of day they where going to have. Whilst some had clear plans and thought they would be controlling their own destiny, others were not quite sure what to expect. The Security Services briefing found Alex McKenzie trying to emphasise to his teams that the best they could do was to expect the unexpected and react appropriately. The previous day had produced more intelligence that added confusion rather than clarity to the operation. Andy Spence and Bradley Bone had met with the Africans sent to North Berwick by Seytan Yilmaz or Harry 'the Turk'. They had discussed taking out at a large scale target at eight-thirty. If eight-thirty was a time, and the conversation overheard by Bill Woods certainly indicated it was, then 8.30pm last night and 8.30am this morning had passed without the destruction of any large scale targets that he was aware of. Why did the Africans stop at the airfield? McKenzie kicked himself for not keeping tighter surveillance on them. Why had they used George Logan, the taxi driver, and why did he introduce them to Ian Steel the hotel owner? What had they discussed with Andy Spence and Bradley Bone and what the fuck was the large scale target on Bone's phone that was to be taken out at 8.30 and which fuckin 8.30 was he talking about? Although he was internally distressed by all this uncertainty he remained exteriorly calm and professional. The phone analysts were conducting a cell dump analysis which would give them details of every mobile number in the area but that would take time and they would still have to isolate Bone's phone which would probably be impossible without some more intelligence. The surveillance teams had not been tasked to follow Bone and he had disappeared off the face of the earth. Real time operational fuck ups were common place and Bill Woods made a split second decision to abandon his search for Bone and follow his primary targets. With hindsight that had been the wrong move but the breakdown had really been in communication. If Bill Woods had been wearing the proper communication equipment they could have followed up their interest in Bone sooner but for a hundred and one reasons he wasn't and they were now retrospectively hunting him. Discreet enquiries with the taxi company had revealed nothing more than he went to Wallyford but enquiries on the ground there had lost his trail. McKenzie instructed the relevant teams on the further lines of enquiry they should pursue to locate him. Andy Spence was now a surveillance target and analysts were working on all his background information. They had found nothing of any real use. The two Africans remained unidentified but it looked like they were illegal immigrants. Their purpose in North Berwick remained unexplained as did the appearance of Joseph Fallon. What interest did the IRA have in two Africans visiting North Berwick? McKenzie was aware of intelligence from Strathclyde Police suggesting the IRA were involved in this plot and that now appeared to be true but it didn't explain why and McKenzie needed to know why. What the fuck was Fallon doing here? McKenzie's head was close to bursting. He had also put a mobile surveillance team on Fallon. That was three teams in North Berwick alone. He had virtually no personnel left. At this rate there would be more surveillance personnel in North Berwick than tourists. Fallon had been accompanied by another male. Some video footage and photos had been taken of the accomplice but the images did not give a decent view of his face. The images were shown to the teams but no one could identify him. Jack Stirling from the covert monitoring post thought he looked familiar but could not recollect why he knew him or who he was. The analysts were left to work on it. Jack Stirling knew he had met this guy but he couldn't think where or why their paths had crossed. Like most law enforcement officers Jack pigeon holed people into one of three groups; family, friends, acquaintances and colleagues being in the first, with criminals and miscellaneous making up the other two. He scanned through the criminal group in his mind but drew a blank. Who the fuck was this guy? It bugged him that he couldn't remember.

McKenzie outlined the priorities for the day. The reality remained that he had no idea what his targets were up to and why they were here. His preferred option would be to arrest them all in the interest of public safety but they hadn't done anything to merit being arrested. Whatever unfolded he had to be ready. A lot of lives could depend on his decisions. He decided to ask Giles Wainwright for some insurance.

Giles Wainwright agreed but he wasn't quite sure why. The whole thing was as much a mystery to him as it was to McKenzie but he requested some specialist resources from his Section Head who made the necessary enquiries with the Ministry of Defence.

Harry 'the Turk' and Serghei had spent the evening as guests of the former Quartermaster General of the Dublin Brigade. The entertainment had taken them to a casino where they had observed a young Middle Eastern gentleman dressed in a Brioni suit, a Turnbull and Asser handmade shirt, a Ted Baker tie and Becketts and Luffield shoes. His outfit was accessorised by an Omega Seamaster watch on a stainless steel strap, Persol sunglasses, S.T. Dupont cufflinks, and Gieves & Hawkes white braces with gold clips. His money which had not been in short supply was contained in a Richard Pell silver money clip. He had been playing Punto Banco which quite literally translated means point bank. In reality it meant two opposing sides, the player and the bank. This game was known as Baccarat in the US and in Asia. Serghei had known how to play and explained that picture cards and tens counted as 0. Aces counted as 1, while all other cards counted as face value. He explained how, a third card was dealt to each hand, If required, according to specific rules. When the point value of the first two cards drawn for either hand is 8 or 9, that is known as a 'Natural' and no additional cards are drawn. Hands don't ever exceed 9 because the first digit of a two-digit number is always dropped. For example, if 5 and 7 are drawn for a total of 12, the count is 2. The hand with the highest point total closest to nine wins. Harry had been more interested in the slim beautiful Chinese girl who was getting upset by her Chinese boyfriend who seemed to be throwing money away betting against the young Middle Eastern player. There were only three outcomes either a win for the banker, a win for the player or a tie on the game. The young Chinese man who was also very well dressed continued to bet against the player and had easily lost over twenty thousand euro. Finally at the behest of his girl friend he had bet twenty thousand euro on the player. The young Middle Eastern gambler had changed tack at this point and bet 5 thousand euro on a tie. Normally this is a bad bet as ties occur less than one in every 10 hands. The golden rule was to avoid betting on a tie even although the odds were substantially greater. Lady luck was on the young gambler's side and the subsequent tie scooped him forty thousand euro whilst the young Chinese player was cleaned out by his bet. The sore gambler stormed off leaving his bemused beautiful Chinese girlfriend at the table looking forlorn and vulnerable. In a manner even smoother than his card play the Middle Eastern victor had offered her his hand and announced, *"The names Bilal, Jehat*

Bilal." A bottle of Bollinger Grande Année 1990 was ordered and they retired to a corner table where they enjoyed its instantly recognizable, dry, toasty taste that connoisseurs around the globe covet. Harry had been jealous. He was quite sure they had also enjoyed a few other physical pleasures as well. He could quite easily buy any woman he wanted but to operate with such style and panache was every red blooded male's fantasy and Harry was envious of that. He consoled himself in the fact that he still had power of life and death over his enemies and later today he would be exercising that authority. He had various options available for eliminating his enemies but today he felt an overwhelming urge to do the business himself. He might not have the sophistication and charm to bed the Chinese beauty but he still had the muscle, bottle and ruthlessness to murder the opposition. He felt the stirring in his loins as his penis became engorged with venous blood at the thought of extinguishing another human being's life. He was a bad bastard and that made him a happy chappie. He briefly considered what he might have done to the Chinese beauty with his erection but his mind soon returned to business. The IRA had purchased some derelict house at an auction because there was a stash of weapons hidden somewhere on its land. These weapons were buried there to prevent them being decommissioned following the Good Friday agreement. No one could previously get unfettered access to the stash because Special Forces and a number of other mobs, including the Chinese secret service were staking the place out. It all seemed a bit strange to Harry. *'Why the fuck would the Chinese authorities be interested in a few guns and bullets. The secret shit involved must be something special or maybe they were triads not government?'* Harry had dealt with the triads before. He was wary of them but no more wary than he was with the Russian mafia, the IRA or even Al Qaida. They were all nasty bastards if you got on the wrong side of them but they were all a lucrative source of income if you had what they were looking for. Harry, Serghei and his IRA friends were going to examine their new acquisition later that day. The present owner, some company called 'Empirical Assets' had agreed to let them start work on site immediately after a substantial deposit had been agreed. Harry personally thought this was very bad business practice on the part of Empirical Assets and he wondered if any other persuasive tactics had been employed by the IRA to secure this arrangement. A number of trucks were presently being assembled to transport the JCB and other equipment necessary to start work on recovering the stash whilst remaining hidden from satellites and other surveillance techniques. For his services, Harry was getting a nice little retainer, first option on the weaponry and a little help with removing Sergei and his Somali friends. All in all it was a nice little deal. The arrangements had already been made with Akhun Adivar, his interrogator to take out Serghei's café. Harry knew Serghei's team would be working late at the café tonight cutting and bagging a few kilo of cocaine which Harry was supplying. The little shit, who was once Joey Carr, had been disposed of and Black Eyed Benji had been ordered to keep Serghei's Somali henchmen in North Berwick for another night. The appropriate arrangements would be made for them in due course. Harry had it all planned. Staying on top meant staying organised and Harry had organised himself a little shooting expedition in the Irish country side courtesy of the IRA.

Mike Shelly was getting frustrated. He had just finished his encrypted Security Service remote conference briefing with Alex McKenzie and he had nothing to add. The analysts had not come up with a new phone number for Akhun Adivar despite monitoring the calls of Jamie Douglas the dodgy Newcastle policeman, Alicia Celik his escort girlfriend or Sally Demir, his podgy informant. Shelly really wanted to pull all three in for questioning but his orders remained that no one must suspect any Security Service interest in their activities. The blue Vauxhall Astra used by Adivar was his best lead but it had not yet been found. Shelly just knew his boss was not happy with the team's progress even though he did not publically show it. McKenzie had also informed him about the disappearance of Bradley Bone, a Newcastle lad who had been frequenting North Berwick and was suspected of having some involvement in the overall plot or more specifically the taking out of some target at eight-thirty. Bone had disappeared from right under the noses of the Security Services and was possibly heading back to Newcastle to take out this target. Shelly was left to look into the Newcastle end of the enquiry and liaise with the search teams in Scotland. Mike Shelly felt slightly happier that at least he was getting allocated proper actions related to the terrorist plot instead of shitty actions to trace dead junkies that were probably just being used to send a message about paying drug debts to similar lowlifes. Shelly pondered the prospect of tracing Bradley Bone without alerting anyone of his interest in him. It would be easier to find the dead junkie.

The surveillance on Serghei's café was still ongoing. The operatives in the covert monitoring posts were now bored with the conversations of its patrons and nothing of any note had occurred since Jamie Douglas and his call girl had occupied a booth. They had a dossier on old ladies meeting for coffee, bosses wooing their secretaries and workmates bemoaning their colleagues but they had no more intelligence regarding terrorist plots. The UK Border Agency may have been interested in the Somalis who supplemented the Romanian workforce but the job was top secret so they may never know. Saturday was obviously a busy day but the number of staff in the café appeared to be a little excessive today. Dougie Stevens was in charge of the surveillance post and he suspected the extra staff members were there for something other than customer service. He urged his operatives to be extra vigilant and keep their eyes and ears peeled. His vigilance paid off. *"Hey boss is that no the blue Astra we're looking for?",* announced one of the camera operatives. Stevens looked and saw the Astra was parked in a street overlooking the rear of the café. It had three suspicious occupants. *"Take the lookout request off PNC, we don't want the local bill involved now"* shouted Stevens. *"Get word to the Op's team that's looking for them."* Mike Shelly was back in the hunt.

Akhun Adivar sat in the Astra with his two henchmen. A quick look at the back door was all he wanted. He would be back later with a few kilos of Harry's best commodity or at least that's what Serghei thought. That was necessary to get plenty of Serghei's boys in to help cut and bag it. He would deliver the goods after the café was closed to the public and hopefully he would deliver a little surprise for the Negro loving, Romanian bastards. 'Time to go' he thought 'it wouldn't do to get caught with a dead body in the boot'.

Benjamin Black was sitting on the front of his boat. His two crew men were below deck. Black was in a bad way with the cocaine but his new colleague Asad was even worse. Black had received word from Harry 'the Turk' that they had to remain in North Berwick for another night. He had squared up everything with the mooring rental. Black wasn't too bothered he hadn't left the boat since he'd arrived and another day of maintenance wouldn't do the boat any harm. It was Saturday anyway and the football was on the radio most of the afternoon and a good part of the evening so pissing about on the boat listening to the football and snorting some cocaine would be an ideal way to pass the day. Asad and Nadif were going back to visit some pub they had visited the previous evening. They said it was a good atmosphere and the people were friendly but Black had declined. Asad was sleeping but he'd need to sort his shit out before he went anywhere. The boy just didn't look well at all. The way Harry was talking Asad's days were numbered anyway and that was another reason Benji was not keen on getting to know him or his pal too well. A quiet afternoon enjoying the peace and tranquility of North Berwick's West Bay would suit Benji just fine.

Joseph Fallon and Michael O'Leary were taking it in turns to watch the Delta Queen and its occupants. O'Leary watched Black pottering about on his boat. There was no sign of the Africans who had gone below deck the previous evening. Fallon was now sleeping in the BMW because he had watched the boat most of the night. The two

Africans had gone below deck last night and the boat had just bobbed about in the bay. O'Leary had slept in the BMW during Fallon's shift and Black's recent appearance on deck had been the first thing of any note that either of them had observed. The Africans were not alone. They had at least one other associate on the boat. Fallon would be interested in that development when he awoke. O'Leary continued to watch and wondered about the next course of action.

Rocking Rab Grantham walked into the County Hotel. The bar was busy and a few of the regulars had already begun celebrating. Whether the celebration was in honour of Rab's birthday or just because it was Saturday afternoon was debatable but Rab was met with affection and kindness in the traditional County Hotel style. *"Hey there's the old cunt now. What was life like before the ice age Rab?"*, shouted Ian Steel.

"Shut it, what are you going to do for a face when Jabba the Hutt wants his arse back?", retorted Rab. *"Give us a seventy shilling."*

"It's on the house pal" replied Ian. The carnage had started. Rab had a quick look around the pub. The

bar stools were full and the tables at the back were also busy. Pablo, Spocky, Bruce, Reno, Flash, old Dodd, Glen, Mick, Billy, Eva, Nina, Donald, Kenny Trish and Pie were all sitting at the tables near the bar. Rab grabbed his drink and joined them. The party had begun.

The Quartermaster General had been on site since early that morning. His men had cordoned off the newly purchased land and began searching the area. They had achieved fairly quick results. He pondered over the complex relationship between the IRA, the weapons and the organisation hired to hide them. Al Qaida and the IRA had been sharing expertise for some time and the Police had already stepped up security amid concern over an increase in suspected Al Qaida activity in Ireland. MI5 had set up a team to monitor suspected Al Qaida activists and supporters in Ireland after the Glasgow Airport attack by Islamist terrorist Kafeel Ahmed, who had been working in Belfast. The Queen's University-educated fanatic had died of burns after driving a flaming jeep into the terminal building. Three Afghan men had recently been arrested in County Kerry after Irish police swooped on a flat in Tralee and found devices they believed could be used to make bombs. The Real IRA and Al Qaida had a common enemy in the British government so it was only natural they should share resources. Al Qaida had offered to deliver a serious blow to the British Government whilst ensuring the weapons cache was never found. They offered to plant a small nuclear bomb, which they had acquired from corrupt officials after the fall of the Soviet Union, in the Houses of Parliament. They claimed to have some amazing technology which would hide this nuclear device from the Brits in the centre of London. All they needed was a substantial sum of money and assistance with smuggling the technology into Ireland. In 2004, the IRA had been blamed for a 26.5 million pound bank robbery from the Northern Bank's vaults in Belfast city centre. Al Qaida considered 10 million was a fair price for the elimination of the Prime Minister and the Houses of Parliament. The Real IRA agreed and the mechanisms had been put in place to facilitate the operation. The wonder gizmo which could hide the weapons and the nuke necessary to destroy the nerve centre of British infrastructure was stolen from the Chinese and brought to Dublin but lost on the very night it was deployed. Four of his best men had perished that night. The very men who would verify the effectiveness of the gizmo had been killed along with the Al Qaida operative who deployed it. It was a serious fuck up which Al Qaida blamed solely on the Real IRA. The price of the operation had been upped by two million but Al Qaida maintained they could still work within the original timescale to keep their side of the bargain. Next week would see the bureaucracy and organisation of the United Kingdom thrown into chaos. The recovery of the weaponry would be a great advantage to the Real IRA when the British Government went down because that was the time to hit them. The big question on the Quartermaster General's mind at this point was if the Al Qaida gizmo was so effective how the fuck did he manage to find the location within a couple of hours? The use of a seismic vibration system designed to detect hidden cavities like bunkers, tunnels and caves had revealed a hidden room under the concrete floor of the main building. There was no obvious means of access but his men would soon dig their way in. The priority now was to get the anti-satellite and surveillance screens in place. In a few hours he would hopefully find his hidden arsenal despite the boasts of the mighty Al Qaida and their super gizmo. The Quarter Master had heard that in different Arab countries Al Qaida was the public slang for a toilet bowl. It was apparently derived from the Arabic verb Qa'ada which meant to sit pertinently, on the toilet bowl. If that was the case their gizmo was as shitty as their name.

The conversation in the County may also have been described as 'shitty' but the patrons regarded themselves as more witty than shitty. Rab was retaliating against the ageist patter coming his way. *"No wonder your stomach looks like a beer keg, It's all you use it for"* he cajoled Bruce whilst tuning his air guitar. He had decided on his Fender Stratocaster in deluxe walnut with a maple neck. If it was good enough for Ritchie Blackmore it was good enough for him.

"Fucking musician" added Donald." *He once tried to write a drinking song, but he never got past the first bar."*

"Aye it was the bar at the County", laughed Rab, as he climbed onto the wide arm rest on the side of the bench which ran along the length of the wall opposite the bar. This was his stage and he was ready to perform.

"Give him a couple of glasses and he's sure to make

a spectacle of himself", offered Billy who didn't think Rab could maintain the balance and poise which would be required to remain on his perch.

"Give it a break Rab, your mind's making contracts your body can't keep. Your belt won't buckle but your knees will and your back's going out more than you do. Get down before you hurt yourself" ordered Nina.

"He's okay Nina", offered Kenny. *"Rab's got a body that won't quit it's just a pity his brain won't start."* Kenny's girlfriend Trish laughed particularly loud at this appraisal.

Rab was undeterred. *"You're only young once, but you can be immature forever."*

Reno joined in, *"forever, aye you've been about forever. They didn't teach history when you were at school, because history hadn't been invented back then."*

"Aye, the Three Wise Men helped him with his homework", added young Pie. *"He's so old his farts turn to dust. Hey Rab, what age are you? When we tried to count the candles on your birthday cake, we were driven back by the heat."*

"Fuck off, I think you should look for a job in porn

because that haircut makes you look like a dickhead", replied Rab.

"Grantham get off the seats. Get down now." Irene's voice boomed across the bar and Rab scurried for safety to avoid the wrath of the landlady.

"Oh fuck the ayatollah's in", muttered Ian Steel. The party continued in the County.

Mike Shelly was watching the blue Vauxhall Astra. It had been parked at a lockup in the Benwell area of Newcastle. There was no way the surveillance teams could blend into the locale so more technical methods were used to track the vehicle's movements. The vehicle was on the road again and appeared to be heading back towards the café. It parked again opposite the rear door but this time Akhun Adivar and his two henchmen left the vehicle and headed for the café. Both of the henchmen, who were dressed all in black, were carrying holdalls. Dougie Stevens was watching the video screens in the covert monitoring station. *"There's a fair bit of activity going on in the café"*, he advised Mike Shelly as he relayed what he could see on the video screens. About eight heavies were in the café, what looked like five Africans and three Romanians. At least two of the Africans were armed. *"I think they're expecting your boys."*

Shelly looked at the boys in question. Adivar had a black hooded top which hung over his black trousers. Every so often his right hand would move to his waist band as if to double check he could access something he had hidden there. *"I think our boys are armed too but no guns have been seen"*, he advised Stevens.

If you worked in the area of law enforcement or National Security then observation and surveillance was the order of the day at the County Hotel. Pablo and Rab had other priorities and they were taking time to enjoy a cigarette outside the front of the hotel. As Jack Stirling watched them from the security services' covert monitoring post they didn't have a care in the world. That was until the local constabulary joined the game. If Pablo had been more observant and surveillance conscious he might have spotted the old adversary who had plagued him during his formative years but a skin full of lager and the security of being on his own turf took away any edge his senses may have had. The first he knew of

PC Pointy Finger was when the finger was pointed firmly in between his shoulder blades. *"Ah Campbell I see you're still a waste of space*." Pablo spun round to see who was trying to attract his attention and was confronted with a bulky unformed police officer in his forties who was sporting an evil grin. Immediate recognition and a taint of hatred spread across Pablo's face as memories of his youth came flooding back. This bastard had worked the beat in North Berwick in the days when the polis kicked your arse or skelped your ear rather than jailing you. That system had served the community fine until one of Pablo's relatives had upset the applecart by trying to change the balance of power and he took the fight to the polis. Attacking the police was not a smart move but jumping in to assist the idiot who started it was a super dumb move. Family, however, were family and Pablo had chosen the super dumb option. PC Pointy Finger had spent the next few years pointing and poking at Pablo with that fuckin finger to remind him exactly where he stood in the pecking order. Pointy Finger had been transferred to Musselburgh or Dalkeith about 17 years ago but now he was back in North Berwick and he was poking that fuckin finger into Pablo's chest. Rab also remembered Pointy Finger and Pablo's misspent youth. He quickly ushered Pablo back into the pub before Pablo could try and re-enact his youthful years. "*Fuckin bastard*" mumbled Pablo under his breath. PC Pointy Finger laughed and began to lecture his young partner about the value of knowing and identifying criminals in the area. Jack Stirling watched in the Covert Monitoring Post as the two policemen walked past Joseph Fallon, a member of a Real IRA Active Service Unit and two African henchmen working for a top North East Gangster without giving them a second look.

Back in the bar Rab noticed that Malky and Watty had turned up and were sitting at a table with Nina and Andy Spence. He ushered Pablo over to the table in an effort to take his mind off of PC Pointy Finger. "*Watty is using his chemistry skills to prepare super cocktails*" explained Malky. He told them how Nina had got the recipe from Ian, behind the bar, but he would only serve one drink to each of them because he didn't want a hotel full of drunks that couldn't bite their fingernails. Drink responsibly was his watchword but Watty had devised a plan to overcome the strict supervision of the tyrant landlord and the illegal chemical plant was now in full swing. Pints of Guinness were easy to obtain. Half the pub drank Guinness so ordering Guinness didn't pose too much of a problem. Malt whisky was sold fairly frequently to locals and visitors alike so it was possible to get sufficient amounts of malt whisky without arousing too much suspicion from the eagle-eyed landlord. The difficulty lay in securing Crabbies Ginger Beer. As nice as it was none of the regulars drank it even occasionally so a sudden demand for alcoholic ginger beer would further arouse the interest of the already suspicious landlord. Watty employed the services of a rather tasty young lady and her boyfriend. *"We need someone to go undercover"*, he explained hoping that the lure of intrigue, spying and of course his own personal charm would bring her on board. Emma Ferguson and Bill Woods were up to the task. After being briefed on the importance of distancing the locals from the alcoholic ginger beer Emma ensured the supplies began to arrive. Guinness, malt whisky and Crabbies Alcoholic Ginger Beer mixed in exactly the right proportions was exquisite and it looked like Guinness. Ian Steel was suspicious but remained oblivious to the reason why some of his patrons were going downhill faster than normal. Bill Woods and Emma Ferguson had joined the scam to get into the company of Andy Spence but so far they had gleaned nothing and were being supplied with drink after drink of a highly potent concoction.

Their ploy to gain access to Andy Spence had been foiled as Watty maintained the importance of them remaining at their own table if the undercover Crabbies ploy was going to work. The irony that the real undercover work had been scuppered by a covert chemist was not lost on them. Watty left the table to talk to Eric who owned the excellent Tea at Tiffany's Café. This was located two doors away from the hotel. Eric's café was renowned for its quality and locally produced ingredients. Watty quizzed him on the quality of the Guinness. Eric had noted that the last couple of glasses had tasted different and wondered if they had changed the barrel. He thought that somehow it tasted better than normal. Watty sniggered and surreptitiously exchanged Eric's fresh Guinness for one of his cocktails. Pablo decided it was time to make his move. Bill Woods had moved to Andy Spence's table and Emma Ferguson was sitting on her own. Emma had caught Pablo's eye the first time she had walked into the County and he just knew she had no romantic interest in Bill Woods. If any chemistry or interest in Bill Woods had ever been there it was long gone. Pablo had been giving her the eye and she had occasionally responded. He knew she had noticed him and now was the time to make his play. Maybe if he had thought about it his timing could have been better but after an all day session on lager followed by a fair helping of Jack Daniels and too many of Watty's super cocktails he felt invincible. He had the looks and the charm. He could talk the talk and he could walk the walk. Emma saw him staggering towards her table. So did Ian Steel. *"Sit on your arse in the beer garden Pablo"*, he ordered, *"I'll phone you a taxi."* Emma assisted and guided him towards the back door. Ian Steel worried about the future. *'If I do sign Stevie Duncan he'll fit in nicely with the other drunks in the team.'*

Asad and Nadif were not unhappy spending another day in North Berwick as it was a beautiful and relaxing setting but they did wonder what possible interest Serghei or Harry 'the Turk' could have in the place. They had spent the last few hours visiting the bars and shops. Now they were standing at the harbour. They would be heading back to Newcastle early the next morning and Benji had asked them to bring him back a Chinese meal which they had just obtained from the Quality House takeaway in Quality Street. They planned to drop it off and hit the pubs again. They thought they might have another go at getting a meal in the

County. They sauntered down onto the West Bay and walked towards their mooring.

Joseph Fallon and Michael O'Leary had been tailing the two Africans since they had left their boat at three o'clock that afternoon. They had done nothing except act like fuckin tourists. Fallon and O'Leary were undecided as to what their next move should be. Fallon was sick of the whole operation. He wanted to search their boat or confront the two Africans and torture them to find out what they were up to. O'Leary maintained they should continue surveillance. *"How the fuck can we watch them if they sail away?",* argued Fallon who was the senior operative and the ultimate decision maker.

"How can we torture them under the surveillance of the Special Branch?", questioned O'Leary.

"The peelers probably know we're here anyway" decided Fallon. He had a plan. *"We'll just fuckin visit the cunts then torture and eliminate them. We can sail away in their fuckin boat and head across the water."* He pointed across the Firth of Forth to Fife which was clearly visible in the distance. *"If we steal another car that should confuse them and we*

will be gone before they can drive around the coast to get us." He thought about how he could weigh down their bodies with the anchor or something similar and dump them smack bang in the middle of the channel. Hopefully they wouldn't resurface and if they remained undiscovered no one would worry too much about the murders. O'Leary was unsure and tried to argue against it but Fallon had the final say and O'Leary had to go along with it if he wanted to remain as part of the team.

Elsewhere other members of Fallon's Real IRA team had successfully gained access to the chamber below the concrete floor of the derelict farmhouse. The Quartermaster General was walking through the basement and examining the racks of rifles, pistols, rocket launchers and machine guns which were stored there. Crates of ammunition and explosives were stored neatly in wooden boxes. Apart from the fact it was a basement full of weapons, ammunition and explosives he detected nothing unusual. He was annoyed, irritated and uneasy about the fact he felt betrayed. Those Al Qaida bastards had done nothing other than bury the fuckin weapons. Where was the big bomb and their fuckin super gizmo that was supposed to stop it being found? His blood was boiling. Their plan to disrupt the British Government better be more reliable than this he fumed. *"Bring down the Turk and that other bastard"*, he ordered. Someone was going to get it.

In the trees on the outskirts of the derelict farmhouse, the unsuccessful Chinese Punto Banco player had exchanged his tuxedo for black combats and a Type 64 submachine gun. This was one of the first domestically designed Chinese submachine guns. It was designed as a special purpose weapon for clandestine operations and it was fitted with an integral silencer. Its sights were of the traditional, open type. The rear sight was a two-position flip-up part, with settings for 100 and 200 metres range. He gave the signal, to his similarly armed men, to begin taking out the guards on the outer cordon of the farmhouse.

Pablo couldn't believe his luck. He had pulled. He didn't even need to use a cool chat up line as his chiselled looks, puppy dog eyes and his charming smile had done the business. *'Emma Ferguson was looking for a bit of rough, a real man and he was just the man to give her one'*, He convinced himself. She had grabbed him and was leading him out the back. His head was a bit fuzzy and his legs were unsteady. *'Fuck am I in love or just drunk?'* He wondered. He decided a little bit of sweet talking wouldn't do any harm and he tried to tell Emma his jelly legs were a result of desire and not drink. Emma had no interest in Pablo other than his personal safety. She wasn't quite sure what he was saying but he had staggered off towards the road and she was worried he might get hurt if he fell or stepped in front of a car, so she followed him. Emma wasn't the only one worried about Pablo. Rab had seen him stagger out and thought he should check on him. Bill Woods had no interest in Pablo but he was worried about Emma and he followed too. PC Pointy Finger who was working overtime in North Berwick as part of a national initiative to reduce street drinking and disorder observed and also took an interest in Pablo. North Berwick was the type of place where the police were expected to look after the public and PC Pointy Finger immediately decided that the young lady in Pablo's company may need some protection. As a result two drunks, two undercover security services officers and two members of the local police service ended up in the Old Parish Church graveyard. Pablo was annoyed, in fact he was raging. He had been led to the cemetery by the lovely Emma who was desperate for his body and now all these cunts had turned up to annoy him. There was that stupid bastard Rab who was climbing onto the very gravestone upon which he intended to introduce Emma to the erotic art of gravestone shagging. PC Pointy Finger had his suspicions about what Pablo was doing in the graveyard and he was sure it would no doubt contravene some law or other. During the middle ages the Church had administered law and order and Pablo would have been glad he wasn't around then. The majority of cases brought before the elders of the Kirk Session, sometimes known as the 'Bawdy Court', were concerned with sex. The most common prosecutions were for heresy, divorce, deformation, adultery and fornication. Shagging on the gravestones would have probably been common place on the charge sheets then but PC Pointy Finger was not too familiar with it. Had he known about it he could have ordained Pablo to make public atonement before the congregation the following Sunday and then pilloried him on the stool of penitence. This involved a metal neck collar known as a 'Joug', which was once attached to the wall of the old Parish Church in Kirk Ports. It was used to hold offenders who had been found guilty of sexual deviance. Fortunately for Pablo this line of punishment was not open to PC Pointy Finger who was also unaware that the metal neck collar had been on the display in the local museum which was due to reopen after renovation. As PC Pointy Finger poked and probed at Pablo's chest and his confused partner tried to pacify Bill Woods who was arguing that they should let Emma go, Rab let rip with a deafening performance on his air guitar. Pablo was still fuming, Emma was trying to hold him back, Bill Woods was trying to extricate two undercover officers from a potential breach of the peace, PC Pointy Finger was having Pablo, his young colleague decided to call for assistance and Rab was strutting his stuff at Woodstock, Stonehenge or T in the Park. The outdoor venue, his gravestone stage, the crowd below as he blasted his repertoire and the euphoria brought about by Watty's super cocktails were intoxicating. He sang *"I've been running Monday, Tuesday, Wednesday, Thursday, Friday, Saturday, Sunday what have I done?"* As he ended the final chords of The Clash and 'Police on my Back', North Berwick's greatest and most influential air guitar player took a stage dive into the crowd to body surf in celebration of his outstanding performance. As Rab crashed into PC Pointy Finger and his dumfounded colleague he became legitimised 'Jail Bait' along with Pablo, Bill and Emma who were now sprawled on the ground after being bowled over by a low flying rocker. As Rab lay beside them in fits of laughter   PC Pointy Finger and his neighbour scrambled to their feet and broadcast another urgent assistant call. Handcuffs and batons were promptly utilised.

Jack Stirling was in the covert monitoring post. He couldn't see the debacle occurring in the graveyard but the story was being relayed by the surveillance teams. Bill Woods and Emma Ferguson were on their own now. If they got the jail they would just have to suffer the consequences. The operation couldn't be compromised for their sake. Jack Sniggered at the thought of the jokes that would be flying around at the next debriefing or the headings on the reports the gaffers would have to compile to get Bill and Emma out of their predicament. 'Body Snatch in Cemetery' was the best he could come up with and he couldn't think of any catchy newspaper style headings about Security Service, MI5, Special Branch or undercover agents. He tried a different tack 'Ghosts grabbed in Graveyard'. It didn't really work. What about a heading with Frankenstein or Dracula. His mind drifted to another funny story he had heard about

Dracula. He remembered this new guy who had come to his station when he was working as a Detective in the Police Force, before he was recruited by the Security Services. The guy was nicknamed FUNG which was the usual tag for a new guy or Fuckin Ugly New Guy until a real nickname was decided. Jack remembered the guy actually had striking good looks so FUNG wasn't really apt. The Sergeant and the Inspector weren't too keen on this guy because he was on a temporary secondment and earmarked for some headquarters job. He wasn't technically new to the force just that shift. They had put him on a big industrial beat where he had nothing to do on the night shift but wander around pulling padlocks and checking that nothing had been broken into. The only place in a five mile radius where any other living soul could be found was ironically in the local funeral parlour. Like the police, death was a 24hr business. The Sergeant and Inspector had tried to catch the cop dossing, which was police speak for skiving, in the funeral parlour and waited until he had gone inside before positioning themselves one in front and one at the back of the premises. They wanted to teach him a lesson about proper policing and reckoned that with their experience at the sharp end they could show this headquarters starlet a thing or two. When they called for him over the radio they were dumfounded to hear he was 2 miles away on the other side of the beat. As they stood there watching the hearse drive from the premises they had no idea how their target had eluded them. The cops escape in the hearse became legendary and his nickname FUNG was dropped and replaced by Dracula. Jack racked his brains in an effort to recall the name of the guy. He couldn't remember. He hadn't been at the station long and Jack had only actually met him once or twice. Rumour had it his headquarters job was in some fancy squad or even the Secret Service. Something clicked in Jacks head. *'Fuck, the guy in the surveillance photo. He's one of us'.* He lifted the phone, Alex McKenzie needed to know.

Alex McKenzie looked at his watch it was almost 8.30pm. He had a large scale drug deal going down in Newcastle. A Real IRA active service unit mounting an assault on a boat crewed by Newcastle gangsters in North Berwick, two of his officers were fighting with the local police in the graveyard and now it looked like he was compromising some fuckin MI6 job where they had an undercover officer deployed. *"Fuck I've got a headache. Get me Giles Wainwright on the phone quickly. It looks like its all happening at eight-thirty after all."*

Michael O'Leary was worried. He was not overly concerned about his own safety, he could look after himself but he was worried about Fallon, his bog dwelling friend, and what he would do to the occupants of the boat. O'Leary knew he was playing by big boys rules and if he was ever compromised he would suffer the same fate these guys were about to undergo. O'Leary had seen it all before. Jump leads and batteries wired to the testicles, drowning, beatings, knee capping, broken fingers, burst teeth and bullets through the back of the head. It was not what he considered the best part of his job but if he wanted to stay in the job he would have to condone Fallon's sadistic pleasures as he tried to find out what these halfwits knew about the weapons plan. He knew the IRA hoped to recover their hidden cache soon but the boss was clear. *"There's a bigger picture. Those Al Qaida bastards are pulling a fast one and I want to know everything you can find out."* O'Leary had worked for years on this job. Operation Chameleon was a big thing and it had taken years of ground work and planning just to get him in the IRA. He couldn't pull out now just because a couple of thugs were due a beating. The information may be vital to the Secret Services too. This job can be fuckin murder he told himself and he focused his mind on the game which would be played by big boy's rules. At low tide the water wasn't so deep and they waded out quietly with their Russian Makarov PB suppressed pistols at the ready. Their handguns were fitted with silencers for instances where conceal-ability of a quiet weapon with reasonable terminal ballistics was needed. This was such an instance. Fallon pulled himself onto the boat. O'Leary followed.

Akhun Adivar and his Turkish henchmen entered the café. The rear door was held open by a Somali gunman who was armed, staring at them, and monitoring every move they made. Another Somali gunman barred their way to the main café area. "*You got the gear?*" He enquired.

Adivar nodded. He had conducted many drug handovers in his time but they were normally carried out in neutral territory agreed by him. Harry had demanded that this particular consignment was delivered to Serghei's café. Harry had even cut the price to entice Serghei to take the delivery. Adivar didn't like it but it had to be done otherwise the plan wouldn't work. The sweat was running down his back and he clenched his fists to disguise the fact his hands were shaking.

"You packing" enquired the Somali.

"Yeah and I'm keeping it" replied Adivar. *"You got a problem with that?"*

The Somali glanced over to the table where the 3 Romanians were sitting. The man in the middle nodded and the gunman stood aside to allow Adivar and his henchmen into the room. *"It's cool man we're all friends here"* the gunman smiled. Adivar noted his shiny teeth and a large gold crown. *'Dental plans for dealers'* he thought *'one day he might invest in some gold teeth himself'*. He focused on the Romanian in the middle. He was also smiling but Adivar noted he probably wasn't on a dental plan.

"Salut" beamed the Romanian and beckoned to a chair.

Adivar nodded and sat down. His two henchmen took up flanking positions behind him. Each of them held a holdall. Three more gunmen were stationed behind the Romanians. *"You guys love the circus"* announced Adivar *"I have learned a little trick for you."* The Romanians looked slightly confused as Adivar stood up and produced five small balls. He began to juggle them. Juggling had been a hobby of Adivars since he was a small boy and he could easily juggle up to six or seven balls but on this occasion he reckoned five would suffice. *"You like?"*, he asked. The Romanians still looked bemused but they had relaxed and some of the gunmen actually appeared to be enjoying the show. The café had been designed to provide privacy. The alcoves were not its only method of protection against prying eyes. The black out blinds covered the windows keeping out light as well as attention. So far Adivar's plan was on track. Phase one was complete. He was in the café, the gunmen's attention had been distracted from his henchmen and phase two was about to commence. Adivar wished Serghei could have been here to see his performance. Serghei would have enjoyed it but not as much as Adivar was going to enjoy the finale.

Serghei and 'the Turk' were at that moment being led down to the basement by their IRA counterparts. They had received word that there were no booby traps and it was safe for them to go down. Harry smiled at the thought of safe. Serghei the double dealing dealer was about to pay for his Somali alliance which threatened his Turkish empire. Round about now his café should be receiving a visit and shortly Serghei would be visiting his ancestors. As they reached the bottom of the stairs they were greeted by the Quartermaster General of the IRA who raised his Brazilian Taurus pt1911 semi automatic pistol and put a 9mm round straight through Serghei's forehead. *"They've got an awful lot of handguns in Brazil"* sang the Irishman adapting Frank Sinatra's version of the coffee song. *"Hey Harry, You fancy a coffee?"* He asked.

Harry was a little taken aback and annoyed by the Irishman's bravado but he knew better than to push the matter. Harry had arranged for the IRA to eliminate Serghei but he just hadn't expected them to do it so suddenly. Harry had hoped to participate in the killing himself in order to scratch the itch caused by his desire for the Chinese beauty in the casino.

"Clean up this mess and get us a couple of coffees", the Quarter Master ordered one of his men.

It has been suggested that men think about sex every seven seconds, coincidently Harry's thoughts returned to the Chinese beauty exactly seven seconds after Seghei's demise. He was reminded of the unscratched itch caused by his desire to fuck her. Ironically Harry was fucked exactly seven seconds later by a Chinaman dressed in black combats with a sub machine gun. A bullet through his brain brought an abrupt climax to his fantasy. The IRA Quartermaster General was not so lucky the first bullet removed most of his gun hand the second bullet kneecapped him and so did the third. Unfortunately the bullet through the back of his head was not delivered until his Chinese captors were satisfied that he had no more significant information regarding the Al Qaida super gizmo which was officially the property of the Chinese Government.

Dougie Stevens was watching Adivar on the CCTV screens in the covert monitoring post. He kept Mike Shelly aware of what was happening via radio. *"It's a circus act, he's stood there juggling balls in front of three guys at a table, it looks more like an audition for Britain's got talent as opposed to a drug deal."* Stevenses' video screens suddenly went blank.

Adivar had been told by Harry about the power cut on his last visit to the café when Harry couldn't see two inches in front of his face and the whole place had been thrown into confusion. Harry had been surprised no one had shot anyone because when the lights had come back on everyone had drawn their guns. Harry couldn't see anyone to shoot and everyone else must have been in the same position. Right on cue as Adivar had arranged the power was cut and Serghei's café was plunged into darkness. The balls Adivar had been juggling with were Infrared Tactical Balls which were highly effective for providing light if used in conjunction with night vision aids. They were concentrical and weighted enabling them to wobble and spin around when rolled or tossed in a room. They were designed always to land light end up, enabling you to see your enemy and leave them at a disadvantage. Adivar's henchmen had been standing with their hands inside their hold alls. Out came Uzi Sub Machine Guns. The legendary Uzi was the most famous and popular sub machine gun in the world. Since its first development, it had been repeatedly optimized, upgraded and developed for special units and special police entities that specialized in close quarters battle. Gangsters quite liked it too. These particular Uzis were fitted with night vision X3 magnification scopes and suppressers which allowed the henchmen to see their targets which were illuminated by the Infrared Tactical Balls and take them out quickly and quietly. Adivar launched the balls in the appropriate directions and ducked down retrieving his night vision goggles as he went down. One of his henchmen took out the two gun men at the door whilst the other sprayed the six men in front with 25 rounds of Uzi 9mm ammunition. The hit was competed in less than 7 seconds. Adivar was now aroused by the excitement but concentrated on phase three of the plan. One of the holdalls also contained a bomb. With the aid of his night vision goggles Adivar retrieved it. Everything was very green with the night vision goggles on. The bomb would be set with a five minute delay to give them time to escape. The recommended spot to place the bomb was located and Adivar began the process of setting the timer. The bomb was designed so that Adivar only had to connect two wires. The live one went to the timer to begin the countdown and the other went into the explosive for the charge to be transferred when the timer hit zero. Both wires were different colours and Adivar had practised several times in daylight conditions. Everything was now green. Perhaps one test run with the night vision goggles would have helped him put the right green wire in the right place. Whereabouts Adivar's mind was in the sex cycle was unclear but seven seconds after starting the timing process he suffered a premature detonation.

Benjamin Black, Panda Eye or Black Eyed Benji had felt someone climb on board as the boat banked swiftly to the side. He ran up stairs. Asad and Nadif grabbed their guns and followed just behind him. The adrenaline was flowing and the tension was flooding through Benji's body but nothing could have prepared him for what he saw. He examined the thick crop of black hair and the circular scar on the side of the guy's neck. He noted the eyes, the facial features and the heavy set frame. He brought his eyes back to the scar. The nightmare that had haunted him since that narrow escape from a Belfast bar had finally found him and he had a gun. Benji recalled the scariest night of his Royal Navy career when he sneaked off his ship, in Belfast, in civvies, and in search of drugs. The search had taken him to the bar where he had been challenged by a big gruff nationalist and in defence Benji struck first. He had never been as scared as when he walloped the bastard with a bottle and gouged the broken glass into his throat. All the way back to the boat he ran in fear of being caught and kneecapped. He had suffered nightmares about the big guy ever since and there he was, in the flesh, with a gun. Benji could see a similar recognition in the big guy's eyes and those were his last thoughts.

Joseph Fallon couldn't help himself. The red mist came down as he confronted the black eyed bastard who had scarred him all those years ago. He finished him with a single bullet from his Russian handgun. Had he thought about it, he might have taken the time to inflict more pain and deformity on the guy who had maimed him but the red mist took effect. In reality he probably never had time to think about anything because seven seconds after climbing on board the boat a high powered 8.59mm bullet fired from an L115A3 long range sniper rifle, fired at close range, went through the back of his head and blew off most of his face. Alex McKenzie's insurance had come into play and hidden behind the rocky formations which shelter the mooring points from the waves were four Special Forces operatives. One of whom was armed with a rifle designed to achieve a first-round hit at 600 metres and harassing fire out to 1,100 metres. It's ammunition was heavier than the standard 7.62mm round and designed to prevent deflections over extremely long ranges. At less than 20m Fallon's Skull was not going to stop a high velocity bullet and sadly for Asad and Nadif neither were they. The bullets downward trajectory took it straight through Asad and into Nadif before it exited, then ricocheted through the hull of the boat. The L115A3 rifle held the record for the longest sniper kill when in 2009 a member of the Household Cavalry, took out two Taliban machine gunners south of Musa Qala in Helmand Province in Afghanistan at a range of 2,475 m. Three kills with one bullet was however a statistic no one would ever hear about.

Giles Wainwright was with his section head in the company of a senior Home Office official. He was being updated regarding the latest developments whilst being berated by his bosses for losing control of the situation and endangering a Foreign Office operation. *"Get it cleared up and don't leave any trace of Operation Sigma. No one should ever be able to link your Operation Sigma to their Operation Chameleon which was a top secret operation. Phone the appropriate Chief Constables and sort out any disasters in North Berwick and Newcastle but keep them in the dark. Offer them a budget increase to cover the costs. They know the score. This is a matter of national security",* suggested the official. *"Just do what you need to obliterate all traces of Sigma and clear up your mess."* Wainwright was fuming at the vocabulary of the senior Home Office representative who had made it clear it was being classed as Wainwright's operation and not a Home Office operation. He had got landed with a shit operation from the Foreign Office and now he was getting his arse kicked for running it. If one of their agents was involved he should have been told! He had no idea what the Foreign Office were up to, but for them to give him an operation which involved one of their assets being in the field of operation and not telling him was outrageous. Wainwright suspected he had been set up to take the blame for this but he still didn't know why.

Crispin Oaksey, the representative of Empirical Assets who technically still owned the derelict property with its own inbuilt weapons arsenal, was relatively happy with the way things had transpired. Seytan Yilmaz or Harry 'the Turk' would not be able to conclude the sale and the Real IRA would have no claim on its assets. The Chinese had cleared up the mess they had made which meant nine Real IRA terrorists and two gangsters were now entombed inside the arsenal. Empirical Assets would pick up the tab for filling the basement full of concrete which should effectively decommission the weapons and bury the bodies for good. A spot of bulldozing and landscaping should hide any trace of where the building had once stood. The Chinese had now confirmed that their missing super gizmo was not located on the property and their submachine guns were now in diplomatic bags heading for China. The set up and the hook were complete now it was time to complete Operation Chameleon and go for the sting. He notified Rupert Basingstoke, his boss at MI6, that it was time to complete the big con.

Rupert Basingstoke was playing for very high stakes. Winning would mean wealth and contracts for the UK arms industry but the consequences of losing were unthinkable. He didn't however contemplate defeat. He was a winner and he had been working on this particular confidence trick for some time. The set up had taken a while but patience and cunning had allowed him to infiltrate and hook his marks. The principle mark was the Chinese. They owned the prize but there was a certain satisfaction in hooking the Real IRA and Al Qaida into the game and setting them up as fall guys for the Chinese to blame. Basingstoke never envisaged defeat but he always considered and planned for set backs. He had unwittingly compromised his own operation by following up his niece's information about terrorists in North Berwick. How they managed to snare Harry 'the Turk' and a Real IRA active service, unit which included one of his agents, into Operation Sigma was one of the little nuances and idiosyncrasies of intelligence work that made it worthy of his intellect. He had dealt with the problem but his missing agent was a concern. Any slip ups now could result in a nuclear detonation in the middle of London which would not really suit Rupert as he was presently sitting in his office in the centre of London and would shortly be retiring to his club, in the middle of London, for a hand of Bridge accompanied by a large brandy. The image of a devastated, radioactive, flattened burning London never entered his mind because Rupert didn't think of defeat. He was a winner, whatever the game.

The Republic of Ireland was famous for its caves and the country was littered with subterranean exploration locations. County Clare alone had 259 recorded caves which amounted for only 38% of the countries total 688 known caves and caverns. The small unobtrusive man from Kurdistan had always considered the cave he was standing in to be a suitable hiding place for his thermonuclear weapon which had been acquired from the Russian arsenal and adapted to suit his needs. The cave was an ideal hiding spot but to further minimize the risk of discovery a little help from the Chinese had been needed. His able assistant, Jehat Bilal, had arranged to steal their latest invisibility technology and then to ensure the Real IRA took responsibility. The IRA's hatred of the Brits had been easy to exploit. Their reluctance to decommission their armoury as part of the peace process made it easier. They were happy to get involved in any plot that hit the Brits and preserved their ability to rearm. The existence of a device which could make their arsenal disappear was what they wanted and the fundamental strategy of any confidence trick was to tell people what they wanted to hear. The British Ministry of Defence had captured the attention of the global media in October 2007, when it announced that it had successfully made a tank invisible to the human eye. The British government was keeping the details to itself but other governments had already joined the race to produce next generation cloaking technology. The British and American prototypes had serious limitations. They were based on silicon and camera based technologies that tried to project images of the surrounding area from the cameras on to silicon panels. A major flaw was the cameras or projectors could fail, and from different angles, the tank was visible. It was a somewhat clumsy and difficult way of rendering an object invisible. The next stage was to make the tank invisible without cameras and projectors. The Chinese were way ahead of the game and not only had they devised more innovative cloaking technology which rendered vehicles, boats, soldiers or aircraft invisible they had also devised ways of de-cloaking the methods employed by the British and the Americans. This technology had been stolen by Al Qaida and was now used to help hide their thermonuclear weapon. It would continue to hide it during its travels to London and up until its detonation. The Real IRA had funded the project on the condition that the bomb was deployed in London and not the United States. The republic of Ireland provided an ideal staging point for the operation and London was a legitimate target for Al Qaida so the deal was agreed. Up until this moment no one else had known about the location of the device. The four IRA men who had brought it here had been totally amazed by the invisible all terrain vehicle which had transported the bomb. Sadly for them, they were eliminated before they could tell anyone. It had not been easy to fake their deaths in a road accident but the British Secret Service were not the only organization that could do this and Al Qaida had mastered it too. The Chinese already suspected the Irish terrorist group for the theft as they were the last link to the device but a continuous stream of misinformation supplied by Al Qaida compounded the illusion. Now three other people were aware of the devices location. Jehat Bilal was one of them and the two Henchmen who were about to help him move it were the others.

Jehat Bilal was a Muslim with royal connections. It was said that the British Royal Family was descended from Mohammed through the Arab kings of Seville, who once ruled Spain. By marriage, their blood passed to the European kings of Portugal and Castille, and through them to

England's 15th century King Edward IV. As a result it had not been difficult to recruit Bilal into MI6 during his university years at Oxford. He loved the lifestyle and the thrill of the work. He was one of Rupert Basingstoke's super spies and saving the world was all part of the job. Saving London was not such a big deal for him. Finally he had found the location of the nuclear weapon but more importantly he had found the Chinese cloaking technology. He was one of the legendary Secret Service operatives who were licensed to kill and he promptly utilised his authority to despatch the small unobtrusive man from Kurdistan and his two Al Qaida Henchmen. Seven years work had just reached its conclusion. Infiltrating Al Qaida, stealing top secret Chinese cloaking technology and successfully delivering it covertly to the British government was all part of the job. As he climbed from the entrance to the cave he activated his tracking device which notified Rupert Basingstoke and MI6 where their missing agent and more importantly the Chinese cloaking technology were located. Five minutes later three British Navy helicopters arrived in the deserted location. Special Air Service troops alighted from the first aircraft and challenged the MI6 Agent. *"The name's Bilal, Jehat Bilal"* he announced and pointed to the cave.

Along with the device it was promptly secured before cloaking technology and nuclear weapons technicians alighted from the second aircraft along with Crispin Oaksey. Bilal briefed them before entering the third helicopter which whisked him away. He had to be on time for his date with a Chinese beauty if he was to continue feeding the Chinese misinformation about their cloaking technology and prevent them learning it was now in the hands of the British.

Back in his London club the news of complete success reached Rupert Basingstoke. He played his card to win the final trick of the Bridge hand. His bidding strategy plus clever doubling and redoubling had insured a winning score to take the rubber. Basingstoke had known he would win even before the first card had been dealt. The thought of defeat had never entered his head.

8 - SUNDAY

Stevie the County Hotel restaurant manager was offering advice to two vegetarian diners. *"Tennents lager is certified by the Vegetarian Society as being suitable for vegetarians. I like it with a steak"*, he laughed. Rocker Rab and Pablo were standing at the bar trying to recollect the previous evening. Watty's super cocktails had numbed their recollection and they couldn't figure out what had exactly happened in the graveyard that had changed their perception of PC Pointy Finger. A number of police officers had arrived administering several kicks to Pablo's arse and the odd clip to his ear. Pointy Finger hadn't jailed him. He had only warned him after administering what

Pablo considered an old fashioned proper police punishment. A kick on the arse and a skelp on the ear might have been slightly excessive and he wondered about the baton weal on his shoulder but it was better than a night in the jail and Pablo appreciated that. Pointy Finger had gone up in his estimations. Pablo was unaware that the order to release him had come from the Chief Constable. He had no idea Pointy Finger was both livid and confused at the order to release his prisoners and possessed no old fashioned values whatsoever. Reduced paperwork and an instruction not to file the mandatory use of force forms had done little to ease Pointy Finger's anger. He had struck Pablo's shoulder with his baton, not his head, as minimum use of force decreed. The normal "Sorry *your honour. I aimed for his shoulder with my baton and missed, unfortunately splitting his head open*" excuse would not have to be used because Pointy Finger's baton had missed it's target, Pablo's head, and struck him on the shoulder. He had waited nearly 20 years for another excuse to split Pablo's skull and he had blown it. It wouldn't have been much consolation to Pointy Finger that excessive alcohol intake had induced a skull splitting hangover for Pablo causing as much pain as any baton strike might have managed. After their release Pablo and Rab had ended up watching a live band at the Golfers Rest pub. Rab had even played a real guitar during the half time intermission. Emma Ferguson and her boyfriend had disappeared. Pablo reckoned she had not been impressed by the police attention and he would never see her again. That was a pity but with the thought that there would be other women, he consoled himself. His hangover would pass and his head would stop thumping. Eric from Tea at Tiffanys, purveyor of quality foods joined them at the bar. He was wearing new glasses. He didn't have too clear a recollection of the previous evening either. His head was also thumping. He didn't understand how he could have gotten into such a state drinking Guinness. On his way home he had tried to clean his glasses when two guys ran past him at speed. Unbeknown to him they had been two plainclothes policemen running to assist their colleagues in the nearby graveyard. One of them must have bumped into him because he had dropped his glasses. He had tried to pick them up but he had been unsteady on his feet and had stumbled forward and this caused him to step on his glasses. As a result they had been smashed to smithereens. Kieran, the barman, lifted a Guinness glass and beckoned towards Eric to confirm that he wanted a drink. *"Naw get me a John Smiths, I couldn't handle any more of that stuff today"*, replied Eric, who was still unsure why his head had exploded after only drinking Guinness. Watty, who had verified his skills in making explosive concoctions, might have found this amusing but he was still in bed with a hangover from hell. His bomb making skills might not have resulted in the splitting of the atom but it had certainly split a few skulls including his own.

Alex McKenzie and Giles Wainwright were also going though Hell. The Chief Constable of Lothian and Borders Police had not been too happy about having to secure the release of four North Berwick drunks who had been arrested as part of a National crackdown on alcohol abuse, never mind assaulting his officers. The report in front of him, submitted by the Home Office, outlined how a member of the diplomatic protection unit was having an illicit affair with a foreign attaché. They had chosen North Berwick as the location of their dangerous liaison. They had become engaged in a domestic dispute in the local graveyard when two passing drunks had intervened to assist in diffusing the situation. The attaché had diplomatic immunity and in the interest of foreign relations the whole sordid affair would have to be swept under the table. The Lothian and Borders Police report showed the matter in a different complexion and squarely blamed drunk locals for attacking his officers. If it was to be believed the arresting officers had showed tremendous restraint when effecting the arrests. The Chief Constable didn't believe either of the reports but was happy the whole incident had been resolved using minimum force and the cover up was endorsed in the interest of diplomatic relations and foreign affairs. It was probably just as well that he wasn't informed about the three dead bodies on the boat resulting from the lethal use of force by the Security Services in his force area. The Special Forces unit had sorted that. On searching the boat they found a number of things including flip flops and two full bottles of malt whisky that had to be disposed of. A quick repair of the boat and it had been driven out to sea where fingerprints and DNA were obtained from the bodies before they were weighted and sent with the boat and its contents to a depth where they would never be discovered. The North Berwick populace remained ignorant of the night's events. The Chief Constable of Northumbria Police had a little more to contend with. Eight dead bodies were removed and disposed of. The official report maintained the premises were empty at the time of the explosion. Five of the bodies, which no longer officially existed, had been illegal Somali immigrants. Three of the bodies had been Romanians. They had been claiming numerous UK benefits but now, as they didn't exist, they would no longer be able to receive the UK taxpayers' money which had been sent to the village of Tandarei in Romania as part of a fraudulent scheme. A ninth body was recovered at the scene. He was dealt with as a victim of a gas explosion. The papers described Joey Carr as a drug addict who had been sleeping in a recess at the rear of the café premises when he was killed in a gas explosion. The necessary paperwork was completed to ensure his body was quickly cremated. The gas board were pacified along with all the other necessary organisations that needed to be blinded from the truth of what had happened that day. The Chief Constable of Northumbia Police was also given a little staffing problem to address.

Jamie Douglas, the community policeman, would never see Alicia Celik the high class call girl or fat Sally Demir again. He would never be allowed to handle informants and would never understand why he was identified for a career in the Traffic Department. He would vent his frustrations on the already over policed motorists.

Theresa and Shemain where devastated when Cousin Seamus was remanded in custody for seven days following his quest for scrap metal from a war memorial. The judge had received some guidance from the Home Office regarding deterrence for scrap metal thefts. The judge would normally have ignored it but something deep down in his patriotic soul was repulsed at the thought of a foreigner defacing a War Memorial. Detective Sergeant Lawry was greatly amused and hoped Seamus would be placed on petition which would mean he would be tried at a higher court with longer sentences and this would keep him in custody for at least 110 days. Despite the court result DS Lawry was still lambasted by his supervisors in QC sub-division for not getting Seamus to admit to anymore crimes. DS Lawry didn't have time to care. Another casualty of the West of Scotland's knife culture had just been murdered and DS Lawry didn't have time to scratch his arse never mind worry about another bollocking for doing his job correctly.

Rupert Basingstoke reflected on his success. Jehat Bilal was doing just nicely feeding the Chinese and Al Qaida misinformation about the deceitful actions of the Real IRA. Michael O'Leary was doing a similar job within IRA circles. Joseph Fallon and some of the Old Dublin Brigade were rumoured to have done a runner with the un-decommissioned arsenal, Al Qaida's bomb and the Chinese invisibility technology. Suggestions were being muted that they were off to Brazil or Argentina. The South American wing of the Chinese Secret Service suddenly had a headache. They knew Fallon was dead but they couldn't admit it and the lead still had to be followed up. The British scientists were unravelling the secrets of the Chinese cloaking technology and the previously believed state of the art British technology which was now technically obsolete was going on sale to Britain's customers in the arms industry. That would increase Britain's returns in the global defence market by billions of pounds. They were currently the fourth largest arms dealer in the world behind the US, Russia and France. Operation Chameleon should cause them to leapfrog the French. It would also increase the value of Rupert's stocks and shares profile but that was unimportant in the grand scale of things. Three organised crime groups; the Turks, the Somalis and the Romanians had been weakened. Al Qaida had been foiled and the Chinese were duped. A total of sixteen dead gang members and one dead junkie were now classed as collateral damage along with ten Real IRA and three Al Qaida terrorists. Thirty dead criminals and a significant pay rise for the UK economy was the result of Rupert Basingstoke's efforts and he was delighted.

A couple of bottles of malt whisky, Namely a Glenkinchie and a Springbank 10 year old were consumed, in celebration of a job well done, by members of HM Special Forces. No one gave any hint as to where the amber nectar came from. Whilst no one in Scotland would bat an eyelid at the prospect of shooting a few terrorists, the idea of wasting two bottles of malt whisky, even in the interest of national security, would be seriously frowned upon. A couple of flip flops had however surfaced and were floating in the North Sea off Denmark.

The Dalrymple Inn was subsequently refurbished then bought over and it became Zitto's, an Italian wine bar and restaurant. Whilst featuring a family friendly Trattoria (*Italian for Bistro*) it sadly lacked a dart board meaning Stevie Duncan was forced to transfer somewhere else to pursue his darts career. Surprisingly he ended up in the County Hotel where the signing on fee was rumoured to be a couple of pints. He fitted in just nicely.

Back in the County Hotel Andy Spence was far from delighted. He was still pondering over the disappearance of Bradley Bone. It was Sunday night darts practice. Malky, Pablo, Watty, Ian Steel and Davy Kerr were also throwing arrows at the boards when he raised the subject. *"I'll bet that bastard is living up with that bird now or he's gone back to Newcastle. He spoilt my chances with the other tart and I gave him money for the taxi. Do you think he'll ever come back?"*

Watty thought for a moment. *"Big Bradley likes the excitement, why would he?"*

"Aye" said Davy Kerr *"Nothing ever happens in North Berwick."*

ABOUT THE AUTHOR

Who is Ethrick Brown?

If you don't work this one out fairly quickly, or someone has to explain it, then you possibly have an IQ suitable for inclusion in the County Hotel darts team.

Made in the USA
Charleston, SC
06 July 2014